# Whispers In The Shadows

## A Paranormal Romance Anthology

### by

### Heather Beck

Diamond Dust Books

This book is a work of fiction. Names, places, events and characters are fictitious in every regard. Any similarities to actual events or persons, living or dead, are purely coincidental.

Whispers In The Shadows
Copyright © 2012 Heather Beck
Cover Photo Copyright © Konrad Bak/Deposit Photos

Published by
Diamond Dust Books

Library and Archives Canada Cataloguing in Publication

Beck, Heather, 1985-
     Whispers in the shadows : a paranormal romance anthology / by Heather Beck.

Short stories.
ISBN 978-1-926990-05-7

     I. Title.

PS8603.E423W45 2012          C813'.6          C2011-907019-7

# Table Of Contents:

# Where Feelings Go To Die

*During the daylight hours, when the sun glistens upon the water and the leaves on the trees sway gently in the wind, one wonders why this serene setting bears the misleading name of Black Heart Lake.*

Ashleigh hesitated before placing a period at the end of her sentence. She was uncertain whether the words she'd written would meet the expectations of her finicky boss. The battle of her mind, pen and properly structured sentences continued.

*So, what is the origin of Black Heart Lake's name? It began over two hundred years ago when a jilted woman murdered another woman who was having an affair with her lover.*

Ashleigh suddenly stopped writing and stared at what she'd written.

*Where the hell did that come from?*

Looking up at the bright sun, its blazing heat radiated upon her face. She squinted, wishing she had her sunglasses. Unfortunately, they had been left in the cabin after unpacking this morning.

Now concentrating on her notepad, Ashleigh erased the sporadic burst of imaginative fiction. She wrote what she'd meant to write.

*The origin of Black Heart Lake's name lies within the fact that the moon, when rising or setting behind the two large elm trees, casts a heart-like shape upon the dark lake.*

1

Ashleigh suppressed the urge to add something like, *when two star-crossed lovers look upon the moon's reflection, they decide to take their lives in the lake to forever be together.*

*Ring. Ring.*

Ashleigh jumped at the unexpected noise, causing her notebook to fall towards the water. She caught her ensemble of some hundred words just before it could topple off the dock. Notebook safely in hand, she frantically searched for her ringing cell phone.

When the cell phone ceased to ring, a cold realization swept through Ashleigh's body. She'd left her cell phone in the cabin.

Ashleigh swallowed hard as she rose to her feet. No one was anywhere near her vicinity, or so she had thought.

Her body remained still, but her head turned ever so slightly. From the corner of her eye, she scanned her surroundings. The extended dock led to nothing but her cabin and trees so dense they created an eerie darkness.

A single breath caught in Ashleigh's throat. Amongst the nearby trees she saw something, or someone, move.

Spinning around to get a better look at the unidentified moving object, she thought she saw a man.

*Weirdo!* Ashleigh thought as she prepared to defend herself.

The trees were still and no sound could be heard. The only motion came from inside Ashleigh's chest as her heart pumped furiously.

The man had disappeared between the trees, but the mere thought of his presence sent chills down her spine.

*Stupid! Stupid! Stupid!* Ashleigh mentally beat herself up as she checked the locks on the cabin's windows and door. *Why the hell would I agree to this?*

It had seemed like such a good idea at the time. Being alone in a cabin; a twenty minute drive away from any human contact; working on a somewhat fantastical yet informative journalistic piece – it was meant to be sublime. Instead of experiencing a heightened sense of self and purpose, Ashleigh was terrified.

*Ring. Ring.*

*He's inside!* Ashleigh thought with a shiver.

*Ring. Ring.*

The ringing was so close.

*It's my own phone.* Ashleigh sighed with relief. *Get a grip.*

"Hello?" she finally answered.

"My beautiful darling, how are you?" a male voice cooed on the other end.

"Upon hearing your voice, *darling*, I'm sick to my stomach." Ashleigh disconnected and then dropped the cell phone onto the bed. Hurt and disgusted, she stared at the phone.

How she hadn't seen Drake for what he really was – a cheating, manipulative, self-centered jerk – Ashleigh would never understand. She had been taken in by Drake's savvy business-man mannerisms. He wined and dined her, yet cheated on her in an attempt to improve his "networking circle." She had to give it to him, at least his excuse was original. Four months into their so-called relationship, the unpleasant truth was revealed. The fact that she still felt hurt was as much as, if not more of, a blow to Ashleigh's self-esteem than actually losing Drake. Although, in a strange way, she hadn't lost him. He still called once a week in an attempt to win her

3

back. As to what Drake wanted, Ashleigh was oblivious. As a novice journalist for a small regional magazine, she didn't possess the money Drake so seemingly valued.

Ashleigh began to undress in preparation for what she guessed would be a long, tense night. Her body ran cold and then hot. She felt exposed, as if someone was watching her.

*I hope I'm not getting a fever.* Ashleigh touched her 98.6 degree forehead.

In her sleepwear, she crept to the window and pushed the blinds aside. No one was there.

The moon was high in the sky, so the opportunity to see the heart in the lake was missed.

*The isolation is already getting to me,* Ashleigh thought, allowing the blinds to fall back into place.

She crawled into the unfamiliar bed and lay awake for hours. Her senses were at an all-time high; even the slightest sound seemed amplified.

At the break of dawn, when Ashleigh had just fallen into a deep sleep, she awoke to the sound of a painful cry. Her eyes shot open, wide and alert, but her body refused to move. The cry drew closer and louder. The cries sounded as if they came from a woman.

Though slow and heavy-footed, compassion and concern drove Ashleigh. Putting on her slippers, she proceeded out the door and through the woods.

Dark clouds hid the rising sun, leaving everything dark and dreary. The chilly air paired with the unfamiliar woods sent unease throughout her body. Twigs cracked under Ashleigh's white fuzzy slippers, and crickets sang amongst the fighting.

"You're a disgrace – nothing but a common whore!" a woman yelled.

Ashleigh ran forward. The furious voice echoed in her mind. She broke through the trees and onto the dock but saw no one.

"I didn't know!" a desperate voice cried. "It's not my fault!"

"Liar!"

The two feuding female voices continued to echo around the fog-covered lake. Ashleigh walked along the dock, keeping her gaze on her feet. The fog became so dense she could no longer see the wooden boards.

Loud groans of women engaged in a physical fight sounded.

Thinking a few yards of planks lay before her, Ashleigh took a step forward and fell into the water. The freezing water, much colder than it should be this time of year, drenched her nightclothes. Her body sank deeper into the watery abyss. Paralyzed by fear, there seemed to be no sandy floor and she couldn't propel herself upwards.

*I'm going to drown,* Ashleigh thought in terror as she closed her eyes and waited to die.

When Ashleigh hit into something hard, she opened her eyes. At first, everything was dark and blurry. Ashleigh blinked, causing her eyelids to feel as heavy as bricks. Something slowly appeared beneath her – a white vision, an angel, perhaps. It stopped her from falling deeper and most likely drowning.

The object came into full view. She opened her mouth to scream, but instead of a voice coming out, water rushed in.

The dead body that lay under Ashleigh had the most awful blue skin and sunken eyes. A tattered dress from the nineteenth century clung to the life-less body.

Suddenly, strong arms pulled Ashleigh towards the surface. Her heart pounded as she felt herself thrashing back and forth between the water and the body of her rescuer. When Ashleigh broke through the surface, she gasped for the most delicious breath of air she had ever taken and then pulled herself onto the dock with a push from her rescuer.

Breathing hard and dripping wet, Ashleigh watched the man who had saved her life pull himself onto the dock. The first thing she noticed was how weird he was dressed. The man wore no shirt. In-stead, a pair of worn-out overalls covered his body. His leather boots thudded loudly as he stood up.

"My love," the man moaned in a painful tone as he extended his arms towards Ashleigh.

Too scared to move, Ashleigh allowed the stranger to hug her. She hadn't noticed it in the wa-ter but the man's touch was ice cold. Ashleigh jerked away.

Looking into the man's eyes, she saw nothing but darkness. She screamed and ran towards the cabin, stumbling several times along the way. One of her slippers fell off, but the cold grass against her foot didn't stop her.

A few heart-thudding minutes of running later, Ashleigh made it to the cabin. Unsure whether the man had followed her or not, she shut the door and leaned heavily against it.

*Thump. Thump. Thump.*

Ashleigh thought her heart would explode as the pounding on the cabin door vibrated through her body.

*Thump. Thump. Thump.*

Ashleigh grabbed her cell phone and called 9-1-1.

"You have dialed 9-1-1. What is your emergency?"

"There is a dead woman in the lake and a man is chasing me! Please, you have to help me. I'm in cabin one at Black Heart Lake. It's at the end of Rural Road 231."

"The police are being dispatched now. Are you injured or still in harm's way?"

"I'm unharmed for now, but he's right outside my door," Ashleigh choked out.

"Is there somewhere to hide until help arrives? Do you have anything you can use as a weapon?"

"I...I don't know."

"Secure yourself in the cabin and wait for help."

Ashleigh followed the dispatcher's instructions. As she tensely waited for help, the thumping continued non-stop and almost became white noise.

Suddenly, the thumping stopped and gave way to the sound of sirens. Then harsher thumping upon the door began.

"Police!" the man behind the door called.

*I hope it really is the police,* Ashleigh prayed.

Shakily, Ashleigh peered out the window and sighed with relief. She opened the door to a uniformed police officer.

"Did you call 9-1-1?"

She nodded.

"I have officers checking the premises for a male intruder. Can you provide me with a detailed description?"

Ashleigh nodded again, but no words came from her mouth.

"Are you alright, Miss?"

Before she could reply, the police officer's walkie-talkie buzzed.

"There are no signs of a trespasser," said a voice through the walkie-talkie. "The only evidence of presence we found belongs to one female."

"No! Check outside the door. He was here!" Ashleigh pushed the police officer aside to show him where the footprints should be.

"But...but..." Ashleigh stuttered in vain.

"Can you tell us where you saw the female body?" The police officer's tone of voice lacked belief. If anything, he sounded very irritated.

"Yes." Determination to prove her words as true overpowered the terror.

*  *  *

The next day, Ashleigh awoke in the late afternoon. Her body ached and shivered despite the cabin's comfortable temperature. The events of yesterday flooded her mind, even though she wanted nothing more than to forget them. Ashleigh had shown the police officers where the drowned woman should be, yet, after a search that lasted into the early hours of the morning, they found nothing. She'd been advised to return with the police to a large neighboring town, but she refused. Yesterday had felt so real, but now, amongst the glow of the bright sun, it seemed to be nothing but a dream.

Ashleigh got up from the bed and prepared to feel the softness of her white fuzzy slippers. Instead, only one of her feet felt a tattered slipper. She looked down at the single dirty slipper with a cold realization.

Ashleigh knew she couldn't stay at Black Heart Lake any longer. If she wasn't going crazy, then what she had seen yesterday was real. Neither explanation appealed to her.

8

*To hell with my unfinished writing assignment. I'm getting out of here.*

Ashleigh picked up her cell phone and dialed zero.

"Operator? Hi. Can you give me the number for a taxi firm?" She paused briefly. "Any taxi firm."

Ashleigh's bags had been packed for two hours, but there was no sign of the taxi. Dusk was fast approaching and, after yesterday's events, she didn't want to be anywhere near Black Heart Lake.

*It should have been here by now,* Ashleigh thought as she prepared to call the taxi firm yet again.

"Beep. Beep. Beep," a mocking voice said over her cell phone, even though she hadn't dialed yet. "Beep. Beep. Beep. It's the man you've always desired. Come and get the ride of your life!"

It was *him.* The voice belonged to the creepy man who had pulled Ashleigh out of the lake.

"This ends here!" Ashleigh screamed with fury.

She grabbed a knife from the kitchen drawer, ran to the front of the cabin and swung the door open with such force the cabin's windows rattled.

The sun had lowered in the sky, and only a few rays of light managed to seep through the tall trees. In the darkening evening, Ashleigh could see the horrifying man. He stood with his arms extended towards her.

"Come to me, my love. I'm everything you've ever wanted."

"Who are you?" Ashleigh shouted.

"I'm Xander, my dear," he replied, while advancing forward. "I'm the man who can give you everything."

Ashleigh tensed up. "I don't know you."

9

"You will soon, my fair maiden."

Xander was close, way too close. Everything about him seemed real. He was as alive as any man Ashleigh had ever seen. Yet, his hollow eyes told of his freakish nature.

Without thinking twice, Ashleigh drove the knife into Xander's chest. Xander looked shocked as he stumbled backwards. His hands flew to his chest as he struggled to remove the knife. The knife finally came out, covered in a black substance.

"You harlot!" Xander yelled as he flung the knife to the ground, missing Ashleigh's feet by only a few inches. "How dare you betray me!"

"I don't know you!"

"You were to be my lover, but now you will become my servant."

"Get real." Ashleigh turned around and ran as fast as she could. If the taxi wouldn't take her home, then her feet would.

"Stay where you are!" Xander commanded.

Xander chased Ashleigh, but adrenaline increased her speed.

Ashleigh's mind raced with thoughts. *Who does he think he is? More importantly, who does he think I am?*

Xander grabbed onto Ashleigh's shirt, causing her to jerk backwards. His grasp was now tight on her arm. Her blood pumped hard as his squeeze tightened.

"You shouldn't have run from me." Xander's breath penetrated into Ashleigh's ear. "You'll pay for your mistake."

"You're full of threats," Ashleigh whispered.

"What?" Xander demanded roughly.

"You're full of threats!" Ashleigh yelled. She wanted revenge on Xander for his obsession with her.

"Stop this, Xander," came a calm but serious voice from behind Ashleigh.

Xander maintained his grasp on Ashleigh and pulled her around as he turned to face the speaker.

Ashleigh saw a woman with a deathly pale complexion and clothing so wet and old it had algae growing on it. Ashleigh gasped. It was the woman she had seen at the bottom of the lake.

"Rebecca, you look horrid," Xander stated.

Rebecca walked forward.

Terrified, Ashleigh couldn't decide which entity was the scariest.

Rebecca reached for Xander, as if to stroke his face gently, but instead slapped him so hard he almost released Ashleigh.

"You did this to me," Rebecca seethed. "You did this to us all."

"But it was worth it. The time you spent with me was the best of your life." Xander was so cocky Ashleigh was afraid she'd be sick.

"No," Rebecca said, harsh and resolute. "Now let the woman go."

"Don't be jealous. You knew you couldn't have me forever."

"You promised me forever, but thank goodness you're a liar." Rebecca looked down on Ashleigh. The corners of her mouth creased downwards in concern. "Xander is hopelessly in love with himself and his ability to make women fall in love with him."

Ashleigh stole a glance at Xander's body. *He does have a nice physique,* she thought momentarily. *Ashleigh, stop that!*

"But he only loves himself," Rebecca continued. "He broke so many hearts, but Anastasia took it the worst. He got into Anastasia's mind and destroyed her."

A flashback to yesterday played instantly in Ashleigh's mind. *Was Xander in my mind when I was writing my article? Has he harmed me as well?* Ashleigh felt a lump in her throat that refused to go away even when she swallowed.

"When Anastasia found out that Xander and I were lovers, a jealous rage came over her. She drowned me in this very lake." Tearing up, Rebecca choked on her words as she pointed an accusing finger towards Xander. "You caused so many deaths and insanities."

Oddly enough, Xander seemed to enjoy the attention. "I was never rejected," he bragged. "Not even once."

"I should have rejected you," Rebecca hissed.

Xander merely laughed carelessly. "It's too late for that, darling."

Xander released one hand from Ashleigh's wrist to grab hold of Rebecca. As he attempted to do this, two bright lights shone on the threesome. Xander was startled long enough for Ashleigh to rip out of his grasp.

"My love!" Xander's voice echoed in the brightness.

"Don't trust him!" Rebecca cried. "His promises and seductions are just lies!"

"Ashleigh!" another person suddenly yelled.

Spinning around, Ashleigh was pleasantly surprised to see Drake. She was concerned, however, to see his car almost completely wrecked. The car clunked before coming to a stop. It was almost supernatural that Drake had made it to Black Heart Lake in that car.

*Why does Drake's presence feel so unreal?* Ashleigh wondered with a shiver.

"Ashleigh!" Drake ran to Ashleigh and embraced her. She suddenly felt very cold.

"Get away from her!" Xander roared with a fury so great that it echoed around the lake several times.

Drake tightened his grasp on Ashleigh. "I have you," he muttered in her ear.

"Xander, it's over," Rebecca said with an unexpected mix of sadness and compassion. "We are not real."

"I'm all man in body and mind." Xander laughed in his usual cocky manner, but he appeared to be growing weaker. He seemed to be losing weight at an alarming rate. Even Rebecca's slender frame was becoming extremely bony.

Ashleigh looked at the car's headlights that shone upon Xander and Rebecca. She and Drake stood off to the side, merely being illuminated by a faint glow. *Maybe the light will destroy them,* Ashleigh thought, extremely grateful that the headlights were still working.

Drake tugged on Ashleigh's arm, pulling her further from any reflection of the wandering brightness.

"We're just manifestations!" Rebecca cried, tears pouring from her hollow eyes. "Manifestations of horrid human deeds that won't fade as long as we still act on them."

"Rebecca. Rebecca," an eerie voice echoed over the lake. "Rebecca. Rebecca." It sounded closer with each passing second.

"Oh dear..." Rebecca whispered without finishing her words.

Drake's grip on Ashleigh tightened. "We must leave."

Drake's touch felt so cold against Ashleigh's skin. "Am I dying?" she asked hazily. "You're so cold. Everything is so cold."

The apparition of a woman in old-fashioned clothing embarked on the scene. However, she was careful to stay out of the car's light beams. Ashleigh now recognized the woman's voice as belonging to the one who had killed Rebecca.

Ashleigh stole a glance at Rebecca, who was shaking. She kept growing thinner as she stood in the light. Compassion filled Ashleigh's heart. *Rebecca's right,* she thought. *This has to stop.*

"With my man, again?" Anastasia seethed. "Haven't you learned your lesson yet? It looks like you'll be making another trip to the bottom of Black Heart Lake."

"E-E-Every night for two hundred years," Rebecca stuttered in pain and fear. "No more."

Xander watched the unfolding scene with great delight but, like Rebecca, he was growing weaker and thinner.

"Come to me, Xander!" Anastasia called with open arms. "Choose me." Although there was desperation in Anastasia's voice, she refused to walk into the light.

"Drake," Ashleigh whispered, "get in the car. Put on the high beams. The light is killing the ghosts."

Drake looked at the car and then back at Ashleigh with wide, terrified eyes. "No, no, I can't."

"What? Why?"

"I – they – we're the..." Drake's voice trailed off as he doubled over in pain.

"Drake!"

The cries between Anastasia and Rebecca continued, but Ashleigh knew she must take care of Drake first. She tore her eyes away from the horrible sight to see Drake covering his face.

"Drake, what's wrong with you?" Ashleigh sobbed. She never thought she'd ever feel concern for this cheating man again. However, something inside of her still cared.

"I was driving here to see you – to win you back," Drake choked out in a hoarse voice. "There was an accident. I crashed into a taxi." Drake began to sob uncontrollably.

*That was my taxi.* Ashleigh suddenly felt numb with fear. "What happened?"

"No, please, not again!" Rebecca cried in the background.

"Anastasia, there's no need to kill," Xander pleaded, sounding as if he finally wanted the horror to end.

"She's in our way, my love."

As hard as it was, Ashleigh kept her attention on Drake. Drake, who was still sobbing on the ground, began clawing at his face.

"What happened?" Ashleigh demanded more out of fear than anger.

"Someone died."

Ashleigh's heart missed a beat. "You killed the taxi driver?"

"No. He's alive."

"Then who...?"

"Me." Drake took his hands away from his face to reveal the darkness that Xander, Rebecca and Anastasia all possessed.

Ashleigh stood up shakily and backed away. Drake reached out for her just as Xander had.

"Ashleigh!" Drake moaned. "I died for you."

Ashleigh ran into the light. It was the only place she felt somewhat safe.

"Don't believe him!" Rebecca yelled. "He wouldn't be like this unless he was a manifestation of dreaded deeds as well!"

Ashleigh looked at Rebecca as she became weaker and weaker. She'd fallen to the ground; her wet clothing clung to nothing more than skin and bones. In the bright light, Rebecca was disappearing much faster than Xander.

Anastasia was circling the light, casting insults and threats to Rebecca while trying to convince Xander to come with her.

Xander moaned and then fell to his knees.

In the distance, Drake painfully called for Ashleigh.

Ashleigh hurried to Rebecca's side. Pushing back her feelings of disgust, Ashleigh gently placed her hand upon Rebecca's tiny hand. "What can I do to help?"

"Leave Xander and I in the light until we become dust. That will end this nightmare for us, but there are so many more broken lives."

"Did Xander really do all of this?"

Rebecca nodded weakly. "Xander may be at the center of this, but we foolish girls are also to blame. We lied, cheated, some even killed, just to be with Xander, just to prove that we were fairer and more desirable than the other ladies." Rebecca breathed her last breath, and then slowly disintegrated into dust.

"Women. I need women," Xander proclaimed as he followed Rebecca into the dusty world of everlasting rest.

"Look what you've done!" Anastasia shrieked. "My prize is gone!"

Ashleigh looked at the pile of dust which was once Xander. She shuddered at Anastasia's obscured way of thinking rather than the dreadful sight. Among Xander's dust, Ashleigh saw a cell phone. By its appearance, she guessed it was ten years old. *A memento from a recent lover,* Ashleigh shivered. She refused to touch it.

"Ashleigh," Drake moaned for her.

There was only one thing to do in Ashleigh's mind. It was harsh, but it was also the most compassionate action she could take.

Ashleigh marched towards Drake, feeling very vulnerable in the darkness. She could hear Anastasia moving towards her with ferocity. Quickly, Ashleigh grabbed Drake and pulled him directly in front of the car's light beams. As she did this, a single clipping from a newspaper fell to the ground. She picked it up and shoved it in her pocket without really thinking. Drake grunted, but Ashleigh knew his pain would soon be over.

"You'll never get me!" Anastasia cackled.

Ashleigh ran to the car and drove forward. She intended to strike the high beams against Anastasia. Ashleigh stopped just before hitting Drake. Although he was already dead, there was something about running over him which was too disrespectful. Instead, Ashleigh watched Drake slowly fade away in the light, while Anastasia took refuge in the darkness.

Ashleigh had fallen asleep in the car and woke up with the engine no longer running and an empty gas tank. Everything was still and quiet. The night had come and gone and Black Heart Lake was rid of two resident ghosts and one newbie. Ashleigh felt sick.

Slowly, Ashleigh got out of the car and stumbled back to the cabin, forever changed.

Ashleigh called another taxi. As she waited, she continued to feel dazed and confused. Everything still felt unreal as the taxi arrived and drove her back to civilization. The taxi driver talked about a co-worker's accident last night. Ashleigh had trouble listening to him after hearing that the other car involved had mysteriously disappeared.

It was an hour into the ride home when Ashleigh remembered the newspaper clipping she had taken from Drake. Carefully, she took the clipping from her pocket and read it.

*Breaking News! An enquiry is being conducted into a possible fraudulent claim issued by Blue Finance Industry Inc. Formal accusations are in preparation against Drake Mark Smitherson, manager at said company.*

Ashleigh recalled the details Drake had told her regarding this claim. She felt neither anger nor hurt upon realizing that Drake's attempted reconciliation with her was probably a mere endeavor to keep her knowledge of the situation quiet.

The driver entered a paved road. It was much smoother than the bumpy pebbles of the unrefined path in which Ashleigh was coming from. She turned around to look into the woods. They stretched along the road, as if trying desperately to conceal what was hidden behind them.

*Why did the ghosts choose to reveal themselves to me?* Ashleigh pondered. *There are so many secrets and so much I'll never understand.*

The taxi driver suddenly hit a pothole on the seemingly horizontal road.

"I didn't see that coming," the driver commented with a laugh.

Ashleigh managed a small smile. At this moment in time, it was the best thing she could do.

* * *

# Hot Egyptian Nights

Hailey gasped for air. All she could think about was relieving her hot aching lungs.

"Miss, are you alright?" an Egyptian male voice echoed in her ears.

Hailey's eyes became blurry. Weak, she fell to the ground. The sand felt like needles piercing her sensitive skin.

"Miss, say something."

Hailey felt some comfort as a strong arm wrapped around her neck and lifted her head ever so gently. A cold compress was applied to her forehead. Hailey opened her eyes. Slowly, her vision returned to normal. The loud ringing in her ears was now replaced with a low buzzing sound.

"You'll be alright." The man supported Hailey for several minutes as she closed her eyes. "Try to sit up," he finally advised.

Hailey did as the man said. Her lips were met with the sensation of cool water. She swallowed, relieving the scorching heat which was in her throat.

"Thank you." Now that the intensity of the illness had faded, Hailey felt rather embarrassed.

"I should take you outside." The Egyptian man didn't bother to ask if Hailey could walk. Instead, he placed one arm under her shoulders and another under her knees. He lifted her gently but also made sure that she was firmly supported.

The feeling of embarrassment began to dwindle. Hailey gave no heed to the gawking group of tourists. She was far too busy memorizing the feel of the man's strong and sweaty body. Unable to resist, Hailey looked at the Egyptian's dark eyes and manly features. He caught her looking at him and smiled. Hailey felt weak all over again, but this time it had nothing to do with the stale air and hot temperature.

The trek out of the pyramid was difficult, especially when one was carrying another person. The Egyptian man failed to complain. Instead, he kept a tight and protective grip on Hailey.

The mid-afternoon sun was burning Hailey. She closed her eyes as a harsh gust of wind blew sand in her face. When Hailey opened her eyes, she was inside a white tent.

An Egyptian man dressed in traditional clothing hurried to her side. "What's wrong with her?"

"She collapsed in the pyramid."

"Heat exhaustion." The doctor administrated a salty liquid to Hailey and then took her temperature. "You'll be fine," he reassured her a moment later. "But you must stay hydrated and keep out of the sun. Tourists like you aren't built like us natives."

"I'm sorry for ruining your tour," Hailey apologized, when the doctor had left.

"I'm the one who is sorry. I hate it when visitors fall ill."

"This happens a lot?"

"Yes. The doctor was right, you're not like us."

The man's words, although innocent, stung Hailey. She studied his face and body, realizing that he couldn't be much older than her.

"What?" he asked, sensing her prying gaze.

"I'm Hailey."

"My name is Zade."

"What does it mean?"

"What?" Zade asked for the second time that day.

"Your name."

"Must it mean something?" Zade didn't give Hailey a chance to respond. "What does Hailey mean?"

"I don't know."

"You tourists are all alike, expecting us Egyptians to be exotic and mysterious just for your pleasure."

*Ouch.* Now Hailey really was hurt.

The silence was tension-filled and awkward.

"Let me escort you back to your hotel," Zade finally offered.

"You Egyptians are all alike, expecting us tourists to stay in hotels. What makes you think I'm not residing in a pyramid?"

The expression of hurt on Zade's face softened. He suppressed a laugh. "I'll take you wherever you need to go."

Hailey raised an eyebrow at Zade. "The Great Hotel," she finally admitted.

Hailey and Zade laughed simultaneously.

* * *

Hydrated and refreshed, Hailey combed her newly-washed hair. She looked in the mirror, admiring her blonde hair and crystal blue eyes. Modesty wasn't Hailey's finest trait.

*Knock. Knock. Knock.*

Startled and not expecting any guests, Hailey cautiously opened the door.

A hotel worker stood there with a small box in one hand and an envelope in the other. "Miss Hailey?"

Hailey nodded and then took the items offered to her. She was getting more than a little annoyed at being called Miss.

"Have a nice day, Miss."

"Thanks," Hailey said, her manners temporarily escaping her due to the surprise gift.

*Who could it be from?* Hailey wondered, while settling onto her bed.

Hailey opened the small brown box first. Nestled amongst a thin cotton cloth was a pendant. Lifting it up by the chain, Hailey examined it closely. Inside the amber oval was something that looked like a snake's eye. More curious than ever, Hailey tore into the envelope. A card, which was decorated in hieroglyphics, was inside.

"Hailey," she read out loud. "My attitude isn't usually so harsh. Please let me explain and make it up to you. Meet me outside Sunrise Pyramid at seven o'clock tonight. I'll be waiting. Zade."


It had seemed like an eternity but seven o'clock finally came. Looking casual yet sexy, Hailey left for her date with Zade.

A hot breeze hit Hailey's face as she walked towards Sunrise Pyramid. Her heart skipped a beat as she saw Zade waiting for her.

"I'm so glad you came," Zade greeted.

"Of course I came," Hailey replied, smiling as Zade placed his arm around her waist. "I had to thank you for the beautiful gift, after all." She cast Zade a playful smile, hoping he knew that the gift wasn't the only reason for her presence.

Zade stared intensely at the pendant which hung around Hailey's neck. "It looks beautiful on you."

"Does it have any significance?"

"Huh?" Zade suddenly looked highly disturbed.

"The necklace – is that a snake's eye inside? What does it symbolize?"

"Oh, we'll have plenty of time to talk about that. First, let me buy you a drink."

Ten minutes later, Hailey and Zade were sitting in the air-conditioned café, sipping on a traditional Egyptian beverage.

"It's good," Hailey commented, after swallowing the last of it.

"Egypt has a lot to offer."

"I can see that." Hailey had to use all her willpower to draw her eyes away from his muscular arms and back to his face.

"How did you end up here?" Zade inquired.

"A crazy life led me to this vacation." Hailey sighed.

"Sounds intriguing."

"It's more exhausting than intriguing. I just want to relax now."

"You're not looking for an adventure?" Zade teased mysteriously. "This part of Egypt isn't exactly a day at the beach."

Hailey realized that she was playing with her hair. She always did that when she was trying to distract herself. However, upon looking into Zade's sincere and caring eyes, she couldn't hold back any longer. "I just finished a degree in new media design. I was supposed to find a high-paying job while living the good life."

"Define the good life," Zade challenged.

"Big house, fancy car, a loyal husband."

"I believe that some Westerners may desire that, but what about you? What's your definition?"

"I'm not sure yet. I want to find the sacred. You know, something which transcends the ordinary and definitely redefines what society considers important."

Zade's eyes sparkled with intense interest. "Why Egypt?"

"The pyramids. I've been in love with them ever since childhood, but I hardly know anything about them. My parents said it was a waste to study Egyptology – what job would it ever lead to?"

"I guess the new media job didn't work out?"

"Not even for a day. Although I stayed at the job for a few months, it killed me inside. I had to get away and follow my dreams."

Zade leaned forward until his lips were only inches away from Hailey's. "A life without passion is a life not worth living."

Desire surged through Hailey's body. She yearned for the feeling of Zade's soft lips against hers. "I couldn't agree more."


"Hurry, Hailey! Come on!" Zade called.

Hailey laughed out loud as Zade guided her over a sand dune and towards a mirage-like shack. Until this point, their date had been enlightening and exciting. But now, as they ran hand-in-hand amongst the warm air and blowing sand, things had become purely exhilarating.

"Hey! Have you got a camel for us?" Zade called, coming to an abrupt halt.

Hailey giggled. "What are we doing?"

"You're going to experience a new mode of transportation."

The owner of the camels took the Egyptian pound from Zade and then handed him a camel. He said something repeatedly, but Hailey couldn't understand him.

"What's he saying?" Hailey whispered, before Zade helped her onto the camel.

"We've got one hour." Zade sat in front of Hailey. "You can put your arms around me."

Hailey didn't need to be told twice. She slid her long, thin arms around Zade's waist and allowed her hands to rest low. As the camel began to stride through the sand, Zade's shirt blew in the wind. Hailey found that a few of her fingers were now inside Zade's shirt. It felt natural as she touched his stomach. It was firm, a sure sign of his hard-working nature.

"Where are you taking me?" she murmured into his ear.

"Do you want me to tell you or show you?" Zade's voice was low but masculine.

"How about both?" Hailey replied, feeling as if she would crumble under her desire for him.

"I want to show you paradise."

"I might already be there."

For fifteen minutes, Hailey traveled over harsh sand dunes on a camel. She was in a place she didn't know and with a man she had just met. However, Hailey had never felt more secure.

Zade brought the camel to a stop seemingly in the middle of nowhere.

"Zade, where are...?"

"Shhh..." Zade helped Hailey off the camel. "Do you trust me?"

"Should I?"

"Yes."

"Then I do."

Zade turned to the camel. "Stay."

"Do camels speak English?" Hailey joked.

Zade didn't reply. Instead, he took Hailey's hand. He led her over a few feet of sand and then stopped suddenly.

Hailey let out a small gasp as she saw the hole in the sand. She kneeled down in an attempt to get a better look. "It's so dark. I can't see a thing."

Zade wandered into the hole. Soon, Hailey could see a flickering light. His hand reached out for hers. She took it.

"Be careful where you step," Zade advised Hailey.

Hailey took the advice but tripped anyway. He caught her before she could fall to the ground. His torch swayed, creating creepy shadows.

"What is this place?" Hailey's so-in-love feeling was beginning to give heed to caution.

"It's the most beautiful place I know."

"This?" To Hailey, it looked like the inside of any other pyramid she had seen.

"Follow me."

"Zade, I really don't want..." Hailey's words failed her as a sparkling blue hue spilled from behind a corner. "What's that?"

"My paradise."

Behind the sharp turn was a pool of blue water. A light from underneath illuminated its beauty and caused star-like shapes to glisten against the sandy walls.

Hailey bent down and touched the cool water. "How is this possible?"

Zade sat down at the water's edge, causing the light from the water to reflect upon his face. Hailey just stared at him, mesmerized by his exotic beauty.

"I don't know," Zade finally replied. "My parents showed me this place when I was a child." He looked very emotional, causing Hailey to hold his hand.

"What happened to them? You can tell me."

"My mother was killed five years ago in a car accident. It was a hit and run by drunken tourists."

Hailey's face reddened. She completely understood why Zade's opinion of tourists was jaded.

"I like to come here and think," Zade continued. "Perhaps I'm looking for the sacred too."

Zade intertwined his fingers between Hailey's. He held her tight, as if fighting an inner battle.

"How can I help you?" Hailey blurted out, not completely certain she knew what she meant.

Zade failed to offer a verbal reply. Instead, he moved his body closer to hers. Zade reached for Hailey's face and then kissed her cheek. Totally smitten, Hailey allowed Zade to kiss her lips. At first it was sweet and gentle, but it soon became passionate.

"Mmmm..."

"What?" Zade whispered, allowing his breath to trickle down Hailey's neck.

"I said I need to breathe."

"Oh."

"Okay, I think I'm recovered." Hailey pressed her lips against Zade's. She loved how soft and warm they felt. Suddenly, the comforting sensation stopped. Zade had backed away. Hailey almost felt like crying. "Zade?"

"I have to tell you something."

Hailey waited, not sure what to expect.

"When I saw you lined up for my tour of the pyramid, a part of me fell in love. Then, seeing you sick and vulnerable, I wanted to take care of you. I can't explain these feelings as anything other than…Hailey, I'm a working man and you're a Westerner who will return home soon. I can't feel this way. I've already experienced too much pain."

"Slow down, Zade. Let's see what these forthcoming weeks hold."

Zade nodded and then stood up. "I need to return the camel."

Hailey laughed. "Next time I'll drive."


That night, it took hours for Hailey to fall asleep. She kept replaying the kiss with Zade in her mind.

"Hailey, Hailey," a faint whisper startled her. "Come with me, Hailey. I need you."

She sat straight up in bed. Her heart raced with excitement and fear.

Hailey had forgotten to close the window. A breeze blew the curtains open, allowing the moonlight to stream in.

Zade stepped into the eerie glow. He wore traditional Egyptian clothing which seemed to swirl and dance around his body.

"Hailey, you have to come with me."

"Zade, how did you get in here?" Hailey demanded as he walked towards her.

"Shhh…" Zade placed his finger upon Hailey's lips. "You mustn't talk, my princess."

Zade stared into Hailey's eyes. His gaze was hypnotic. Hailey felt overwhelmed by the urge to let herself go. She closed her eyes and breathed deeply. Hailey was asleep before she had a chance to exhale.


"Awake, my beauty, awake."

Hailey's eyes fluttered open. The air was hot and stale. Her throat burned and her skin felt like sandpaper. She tried to sit up but she couldn't. It took her a few moments but she finally realized that she was lying on a stone table.

"Hailey."

Hailey tried to turn her head, but she was unable to do so.

"It won't take long," Zade said, leaning over her.

*What won't take long?* Hailey silently cried since she couldn't move her lips.

"The sacrifice," Zade replied, after reading her mind. "I just need your heart."

*Please, no!* Hailey's body would have shaken in fear if it weren't frozen on the table.

"It won't hurt..." Zade tittered, "much!"

*You're nuts!*

"On the contrary, my dear; I'm actually quite sane. I'll tell you what would be insane – allowing fresh sacrificial blood like yours to escape."

*You overzealous freak!*

"I do like to please the Great Pharaoh, but I'm more interested in what he can do for me." Zade brought his face closer to Hailey's. "Look at me. Look at what I really am."

Hailey had to suppress the urge to throw up as she stared at his face. His once attractive features had turned to decaying flesh. Zade was a mummy. A walking, talking, mentally unstable mummy.

"No comment?" Zade reacted with a surprising amount of passion. "I am the man you will serve once I make you a mummy. A ten thousand-year-old mummy needs to replenish himself somehow!"

Zade faded from Hailey's view only to return a moment later. This time he held a long, pointy dagger.

*Please, Zade, you can't!*

"Oh, but I can!" Zade ripped the neckline of Hailey's nightshirt. He then recoiled in horror.

Hailey felt a deep neckline of sweat-ridden cloth removed from her sticky body. *What's with the disgust, boy? I'm amply endowed!*

"Where...where did you get that?"

*Excuse me? They're real, idiot!*

"The pendant!" Zade shrieked.

Hailey looked down at her chest. It wasn't as exposed as she thought it would be. "Hey! I'm free!" As if by magic, she was able to move. She quickly jumped up from the stone table.

Zade had lost control of her and he knew it. "Hailey, my dear, that pendant will render you dead."

Hailey looked at her necklace. "You gave me poisoned jewelry?"

Zade was taken aback. "Ah, of course," he recovered quickly. "But I've changed my mind. Give it back to me."

"What happens if I don't?" Hailey discreetly looked around the sandy room. She was sure that she was in a pyramid. Unfortunately, she couldn't see an exit. The room was poorly lit by only one torch that stood beside the stone table.

"The Viper's Eye is draining your strength," Zade pleaded. "Don't you feel it?"

"I do feel a bit weak," Hailey admitted.

"Take it off. Give it to me."

"Why do you want it so badly?" she challenged.

"Give it to me!"

Zade's yell was so fierce that Hailey's hands immediately went to the clasp on the necklace. She gasped. The clasp was no longer there. Hailey moved her fingers around the chain, but there was no way to remove the necklace.

"It...it won't come off," Hailey stuttered.

"What do you mean?" Zade reached for the necklace but then pulled his hand back. He looked terrified at the mere thought of touching it.

Hailey suddenly decided that she should keep the necklace close to her. "I said I can't."

Zade looked suspicious. "Cover it up then." He looked into Hailey's eyes. The mysterious gaze left her completely under his control.

Hailey pulled her nightshirt over the necklace. She felt her body become stiff. Her ripped nightshirt fell from her grasp, revealing the necklace. Again, Hailey was released from his spell. She now understood that the exposed necklace made her resistant to Zade's power.

"Why are you stopping?" Hailey tested Zade. "I thought you needed to save me from the necklace." Hailey raised an eyebrow. She knew she had the sneaky mummy trapped.

Zade's mummified mouth creased into a frown. "I don't want to create a mummy from such a beautiful lady, but I need your heart to live."

"You're not living, Zade! You're a dead fraud!" Hailey took a deep breath. "Kill me. Go right ahead and kill me."

In a fury, Zade charged towards her. He attempted to plunge the dagger into her heart but was stopped by the necklace. The Viper's Eye shone brightly, causing a protective shield of light to engulf Hailey.

Zade was more furious than ever. Hailey watched him with a new sense of wonderment.

"Why did you give me the necklace?" Although her heart was racing, Hailey wasn't surprised to discover that the necklace held great powers. After everything she'd been through tonight, nothing seemed impossible.

Zade remained silent, as if contemplating his next move.

Bravely, Hailey stepped towards him. "You're a mummy but that's not all. You're also the man who lived ten thousand years ago. You gave me this necklace as a man because you knew it would protect me when you became the mummy."

Zade looked temporarily confused, but then he smiled. "You know me so well."

"Be the man you were. Let me go."

"Alright. Follow me."

Hailey's heart soared. She was ecstatic that she'd talked some sense into the cursed but somewhat humane mummy.

Zade reached for the torch. It flickered as he walked. "Stay close to me."

Hailey did as Zade said, even though the smell of his decaying flesh was almost unbearable. *I wonder if he'll fully disintegrate without my heart.*

The shadowy concaves concealed an exit. The path was narrow, but Hailey managed to squeeze through. The path began to slop downwards. A new smell entered her senses, but she couldn't decipher what it was.

"Does this lead outside?" Hailey asked anxiously.

"Yes. Trust me."

The unidentified smell grew stronger and the intensity of the heat increased. Zade grabbed Hailey with his bony hand and pulled her into a dark room. Hailey cried for help, but no one could hear her.

"You'll burn until the Viper's Eye is gone and then I'll have your heart!"

For such a fragile-looking mummy, Zade had a tight grip on Hailey as he continued to push her forward. From the faint light of his torch, Hailey could see a pool of bubbling tar.

"Zade, please! Remember your humanity!"

Zade snorted. "You're delusional." He pushed her until she was just inches away from the tar. Being so close to it made her skin tingle and sweat.

"Viper's Eye. Viper's Eye. Please save me," Hailey chanted in desperation.

"Shut up. Life as you know it is over."

"Viper's Eye. Viper's Eye."

The light from the Viper's Eye began to shine. It was faint at first but then grew in intensity.

Zade swore as he was forced to release Hailey. He was stunned by the power of the Viper's Eye and the unbreakable spell it had cast.

Thinking quickly, Hailey grabbed Zade and shoved him towards the boiling tar. His resistance was unsuccessful as he landed in the tar with a sickening splash. Hailey watched him sink in the pool of tar. It engulfed his body as he withered away.

"I'm sorry, Zade," Hailey muttered, "but I couldn't let you live like that."

A few minutes later, the shaken-up Hailey was trekking through the pyramid. During her struggle with Zade, the torch had fallen to the ground and lost its flame. Now, she ran her hand over the sandy wall in an attempt to navigate her way to freedom. From her best estimation, she had made it back to the room she'd awakened in.

Hailey felt her way around the perimeter of the room. She was on the verge of tears when her fingers felt the entrance. There was a gap much smaller than the path she had originally come through. Dehydrated and weak, the last thing she wanted to do was squeeze through a gap which could lead any-where. The alternative, which was to stay where she was and die, didn't sound much better.

Hailey chose to move forward but was hardly able to get through the narrow path. The sand scraped her skin like the ultimate exfoliation. The path became smaller. Hailey was sure she would for-ever be trapped between the sandy walls.

A gust of air whipped Hailey's face. One last push and she was free from the dreadful pyramid.

*Thank goodness,* Hailey thought.

Although Hailey had escaped from the pyramid, she still had to conquer the wide open desert.

Hailey felt like crying as she struggled through the sand. The moon was partially covered by clouds so she could hardly see where she was going. As if Hailey was seeing a mirage, a man riding a camel ad-vanced towards her. Picking the better of two bad options, she waved for his attention.

The man saw her and hurried his camel forward.

"Can you take me to the Great Hotel?" Hailey shouted like a fool. The last word caught in her throat. The man on the camel was Zade.

"Hailey!" Zade cried.

Hailey backed away in fear. "No, it can't be."

"Oh, Hailey!" a modern dressed Zade cried as he jumped off the camel and attempted to embrace her.

Hailey recoiled in horror. "No, you're dead!"

Zade was shocked by Hailey's words. "You've found out already?"

"I figured it out when you tried to kill me!"

Zade looked at the exhausted and traumatized Hailey. "Let me take you to the hotel. We can talk there."

"Let go of me!" Hailey pulled her arm from Zade's grasp.

"Please, Hailey. I think I know what happened. The man you were with wasn't me."

"I believed that once – before you tried to push me into the boiling tar!"

Zade felt ill. "Tell me he didn't take your heart."

"You're a psychopath!" Hailey turned around and then proceeded to run. Everything felt as if it was happening in slow motion as she fell to the ground and blacked out.

When Hailey woke up, she was in her hotel room. *I should have asked for the second floor,* she thought groggily as a breeze caressed her body.

"Actually, I used the key under the mat." Zade paused for a moment. "Sorry. I usually don't read people's minds."

"Like it's stopped you before."

"Hailey, that wasn't me." Zade sat on the bed next to her.

"I know what you are," Hailey said. Before to-night, she would have been delighted to have Zade so close, but now she was terrified. It was shocking how so little time could change so much.

"You don't...not really," Zade protested. "Tell me what happened to you tonight."

"Go to hell."

"Said got to you, didn't he? He tried to take your heart, but the Viper's Eye saved you."

"And now you're back from the dead to finish the job," Hailey seethed.

"Where is Said now?"

"Right in front of me."

"He's my twin brother, Hailey." Zade stopped speaking to clear his throat. It looked as if he was about to cry. "Our father ruled Egypt ten thousand years ago. My whole family was killed in an insurgence, but we didn't perish. The Great Pharaoh from above granted us to live for eternity. After a few hundred years, my father and brother became jaded. They began killing civilians just for the thrill of it. The Great Pharaoh was disturbed by this and summoned them into mummies. My father and brother found a way to survive though. They took the hearts of others so they could appear sporadically in human form. I thought Said might come after you, so I gave you the Viper's Eye. Its power of protection is great."

"I know." Hailey looked at the necklace. The Viper's Eye was sparkling. *He must be telling the truth. Otherwise, he wouldn't have given me the Viper's Eye.* "Okay, I believe you." Hailey suddenly found herself even more attracted to Zade.

Zade smiled widely and then hugged Hailey. "Thank you for trusting me."

"What about yourself and your mother?"

"We both held onto our sanity. But you know what happened to my mother. I guess the pharaoh's gift didn't extend to protection against man-made things."

Hailey nodded sadly. "And your father?"

"He was killed by a mummy hunter." Zade was suddenly filled with rage. "My father was wrong, but so was the hunter. A death for a death never results in equilibrium."

Hailey swallowed hard. She had a sinking feeling about where their conversation was heading.

"Where is my brother now? I need to talk to him again. I believe I can make him change."

"I...I..."

"Hailey, what happened with Said?"

Hailey's mind raced. She could tell Zade that she'd destroyed Said, thus leaving him infuriated with her. Or she could lie and bask in Zade's masculinity for as long as possible.

Hailey plastered a wide smile upon her face. "Said broke down and said he had to leave this city. He wanted to start over."

A look of relief washed over Zade's face. "Oh, thank goodness!"

As he hugged her gratefully, Hailey wondered if Zade still had a brain.

* * *

# Rival To Survival

*Present Day...*

It was like the storm came out of nowhere. The warm and somewhat sunny day had been pleasant, so Scarlet thought the night would be like any other. Unfortunately, her presumption couldn't be further from the truth.

There was no light rain before the storm to foretell of the approaching disaster. It started with heavy drops of rain which could easily be seen and heard, and thus mistaken for hail. Then the lightning and thunder began.

Scarlet had been sitting in the living-room, swaying ever so gently in a wicker-chair. She was reading a book. That's what Scarlet usually did when Harv was out hunting for the magical mushrooms.

Scarlet closed the windows before the water could get inside. She then went to comfort Blackie because her dear cat always hated thunderstorms. Scarlet's heart ached when she remembered that Blackie was no longer with them.

*Just like everything else, habits die hard,* Scarlet thought, slightly bitter. *That's why Harv does this. There would only be pain if we were to lose one another.*

It hardly seemed possible, but the storm got worse. "What-if" scenarios plagued Scarlet's mind. *What if Harv got lost? What if someone has hurt him? No,*

Scarlet's rationality replied. *Harv knows these woods and he's stronger than any man I've ever known.*

The minutes passed tensely as the storm raged on. Walking back and forth and constantly pulling the curtains aside to look out the window only increased Scarlet's anxiety. She took one last look out the window to see nothing but wet trees shaking in the harsh wind.

*Harv, come back to me,* Scarlet silently begged as she ran to the only place that could give her comfort during Harv's absence.

In the bedroom she shared with Harv, Scarlet cast the single sheet aside and then climbed into bed. When she used to live in the city, she would always make her bed. There would be a sheet, blanket and quilt. Scarlet always did this, even in summer. Now that Scarlet lived with Harv, things were different. Their log cabin was lovely and presentable, but keeping up appearances was no longer crucial. There were other things to concentrate on and to worry about.

Scarlet lay on the bed and pulled the sheet tightly around her. She pushed her pillow aside and used Harv's instead. Scarlet buried her face into his pillow, smelling the scent which he had left behind.

"Oh, Harv," Scarlet muttered painfully at the mere thought of never seeing him again. *After all our work, to lose you would be a tragedy.*

Scarlet began to cry. The pain she had always wanted to avoid rushed over her like a caged animal suddenly let loose.

Heavy-eyed and out of tears, Scarlet began to fall asleep half an hour later. Moments after her eyes closed in preparation for slumber, her half-conscious mind whispered to her, "Do you know how much you're loved?"

The thunder roared like the pangs of childbirth, but Scarlet was now oblivious to its cries. She was in dreamland; a place where the unearthly was plausible. Yet, Scarlet's dreams could never supersede the life she led in reality. That night Scarlet didn't just dream – she experienced a reoccurrence from a time not so long ago.

\* \* \*

*Late May...*

It was the last semester in Scarlet's final year at university. Four years of undergraduate stressing and studying had led to this moment. She was about to sit her last exam.

"I know this material," Scarlet said as she closed her scribble-filled notebook for the last time. "I hope."

"Good luck," Scarlet's friend commented as she stood up.

The nervous students began filing into the examination room.

Scarlet rose. "Good..." she began to return the blessing. However, her words were cut short as someone crashed into her.

She let out a gasp as she fell back onto the bench. Her notebook skidded across the floor.

"I am so sorry," a man hurried to say.

Scarlet looked up to see a pair of intense blue eyes staring at her in concern. Slightly uncomfortable, she backed away.

Sensing her discomfort, the man moved back also. This allowed Scarlet to see him better. He was an impressive height, standing just less than six foot five. He was well-built and dressed in a manner that required taste and money.

"I'm so sorry," the man repeated as he quickly grabbed Scarlet's notebook and handed it to her.

Some students stopped to stare and snicker. Scarlet's friend, sensing that something was happening, left the two strangers alone.

"Um, thanks," Scarlet said, upon receiving her notebook.

"I didn't see you," the man hurried to explain. He stopped speaking to laugh.

"What?" Scarlet demanded, feeling even more self-conscious.

"I crashed into you, and you said thanks."

"My head's not with reality. I've got an exam like right now."

The man's face fell. "I didn't hurt you, did I?" he asked in a panic. "Your hand, it's alright to write with, I hope."

"It's fine." With that said, Scarlet got up and hurried towards the examination room.

"It was nice running into you," the man said, causing her heart to skip a beat.


Scarlet exited the examination room three hours later. Her eyes were blurry and her back was sore. However, she wore a wide smile upon her face. She'd finished the exam and was sure she'd done well.

*It's all over,* Scarlet thought with relief and just a hint of sadness.

"How did it go?"

Scarlet jumped upon hearing the voice. She looked sideways to see the man who had literally ran into her.

"Hi," was all Scarlet could say.

"Did the exam go well?" the man asked, stepping closer to Scarlet.

"It went great," Scarlet smiled, while feasting upon his sexy eyes and masculine scent.

"That's good to hear."

*What's he doing here?* Scarlet asked herself with a racing heart. She smoothed her hair and straightened her shirt. Scarlet reddened slightly when she realized that the man was still watching her.

"I was hoping to see you again," he said, as if reading her mind.

Scarlet experienced a surge of self-confidence. "I was hoping to see you again too."

"Really?" The man smiled widely.

Scarlet nodded, while casting him what she hoped was a sexy glance.

"In that case, would you like to grab a bite to eat?"

"I'm starving," Scarlet admitted.

"Then let's do something about it." The man offered his arm to Scarlet. She didn't hesitate in taking it.

*He's debonair yet casual,* Scarlet thought in admiration.

"I'm Trevor, by the way."

"Scarlet."

"A crimson girl, huh?" Trevor joked as he stole a glance at Scarlet.

"No." Scarlet paused slightly to pique intrigue. "I'm a crimson *woman*."

"You certainly are," he laughed.

\* \* \*

*Late August...*

Scarlet had always thought university was tough, but the real challenge came after graduation. Searching for a job in correlation with an English degree was anything but easy.

Among the quest for full-time employment was Trevor. Scarlet spent several hours with him each day. He was smart, gorgeous and caring – overall a perfect gentlemen.

All of Scarlet's friends told her how lucky she was to have a man like him. Most of the time, she would agree. Trevor was the epitome of a perfect boyfriend, yet, sometimes late at night while Scarlet lay awake, she had the feeling that something was missing in her life.

"Thanks for agreeing to this movie," Scarlet said.

It was almost 5 p.m. on Monday as she started the rented chick flick.

"Anything for my lady." Trevor smiled at Scarlet and then kissed her gently upon the lips. The sensation was warm and soft.

*Trevor's amazing. How could I ever think differently?* Scarlet scolded herself.

The previews had just begun as Scarlet and Trevor settled comfortably onto the couch.

*Ring. Ring.*

"Hello?" Scarlet answered the ringing telephone.

"May I speak to Scarlet?" the person on the line inquired.

"This is she."

"Hello, Scarlet. It's Karyn from Hot Spot Magazine."

"Hi, Karyn," Scarlet replied, her heart rate increasing. She'd had an interview at Hot Spot Magazine for an editorial position. It was a presumptuous move on Scarlet's part, but she believed she had the skills to do the job well.

"I'm happy to tell you that your resume and interview blew us away. We would be honored to add you to our magazine's staff."

Scarlet was almost speechless. "Thank you," she finally managed to say.

After receiving further details, Scarlet hung up. She turned to an expectant Trevor. "I got the job!" she exclaimed excitedly.

Trevor lifted Scarlet up and twirled her around.

Everything in Scarlet's life suddenly seemed complete.

\* \* \*

"Thanks for the ride, but I could have driven myself," Scarlet stated.

"Highway 28 is so fast and curvy," Trevor replied as he turned off the car's engine. "And you're nervous about your first day at work. I just wanted to make sure that you arrived..."

Trevor was unable to finish his sentence as Scarlet placed her lips harshly against his. The kiss lasted until Trevor was gasping for air.

"Whoa. Where did that come from?" he asked with a laugh.

"You're sweet, but I can take care of myself."

"I know," Trevor said with a twinkle of excitement in his eyes. "You're a woman."

Scarlet suddenly felt her stomach churn. "I better get inside," she said quickly.

Trevor held onto Scarlet's arm, stopping her from exiting the car. "Knock 'em dead."

She forced herself to smile. "Don't I always?"

Scarlet stared at the tall office building which loomed above her. She could hear Trevor's car drive away.

*Man, who would have thought I'd be so nervous?* Scarlet pondered, before taking the first step towards her new life.

* * *

*Early September...*

*It's amazing how fear can so quickly dissipate,* Scarlet thought as she edited an article for what seemed like the hundredth time. *Boredom is a killer to all.*

Scarlet had been working at Hot Spot Magazine for over a week now. At first, she had been overjoyed at editing articles. It instilled in her the feeling of power, as if she was an essential part of a creative endeavor. Now, however, replacing semicolons with periods was just plain tedious.

"I told you to clean the offices *before* the cubicles!" a woman suddenly yelled.

*Excitement!* Scarlet thought, her head rising up from the article she was working on.

"We have schedules here. I suggest you follow them or get out!"

Scarlet furrowed her eyebrows. *That's Karyn,* she realized. *How uncharacteristic.*

Scarlet heard footsteps approaching. She quickly pretended to turn her attention back to the article. Keeping her head down, Scarlet's eyes traveled upwards to see Karyn storm past.

Everything was silent once again. Moments later, Scarlet could hear a faint and undecipherable noise. Boredom and curiosity got the better of her as she rose from her seat and peeked out the office door.

In the distance she saw the profile of a man. He appeared to be organizing the cleaning trolley which stood in front of him.

She let out a small gasp as the man accidentally knocked a bottle off the trolley. Liquid spilled onto the floor.

Scarlet was sure this was the person Karyn had yelled at. *Poor thing,* she thought sympathetically.

"Excuse me!" Scarlet called, hurrying from her office in aid of the cleaning man.

The man jumped upon hearing Scarlet's voice. He turned quickly, worry blazing in his eyes. As soon as the man saw Scarlet, his expression softened. His body relaxed and his eyes suddenly looked glazed.

"I'm sorry to scare you," Scarlet said as her eyes feasted upon the man. He was a medium height and build. He had short light brown hair and three day stubble upon his face. The man wasn't extraordinarily good-looking, but there was just something about him.

Scarlet had been staring at the man for so long that everything else became blurry. The man didn't mind Scarlet's stare since he was doing the same to her.

"The liquid!" Scarlet hurried to say, finally remembering the reason she was in the hall.

"Oh." The man quickly grabbed a towel from the trolley to soak up the liquid.

Scarlet bent down next to the man. There was something drawing her close to him. She took the towel from the man and pressed it hard against the wet floor.

"What was in the bottle?" Scarlet asked.

"Just water. I use it for the plants."

The man got another towel and worked on cleaning the mess. There wasn't a moment of silence in their conversation.

"Thanks for helping me. The other workers always ignore me."

The man's words sounded too open for a new acquaintance, but Scarlet didn't care.

"It's their loss then."

"That's kind of you to say," the man noted.

"It's the truth. Why haven't I seen you before?"

"I don't know," he replied. "Why haven't I seen you before? I'd always remember your face, so I know you're new here."

As they talked, Scarlet and the man moved closer to each other.

Panic suddenly struck Scarlet. *What the hell is happening here?*

Scarlet quickly stood up. The man looked distraught to see her do so. Nevertheless, he followed her actions.

"Karyn is usually nicer." Scarlet didn't know what else to say.

"She treats me like dirt. I guess that's because I clean it."

Scarlet felt her face flush in anger. "Don't belittle yourself," she snapped, feeling the odd sensation of simultaneously wanting to control him but also see his true self.

"I was having a rough day…"

"Scarlet," she blurted out her name, hoping to receive his in return.

"Harv."

"I...I have to go," Scarlet stuttered, hurrying from the hall and into her office. She shut the door and then locked it.

Scarlet sat in her chair. Her heart and head were pounding. She felt torn but happy. It was the closest she had ever gotten to a sublime experience.

"Did you have a nice day at work?" Trevor asked her later that night.

It was a simple question, but Scarlet hardly knew how to answer it.

"Sure," Scarlet finally replied. "How was your day?"

Scarlet and Trevor talked on the telephone for over an hour, but her mind wasn't in the conversation. All she could think about was Harv.

* * *

*Middle of September...*

Loyalty got the better of Scarlet. She and Trevor had been dating for almost four months now. Scarlet felt like it was her duty to stick by him.

*Anyway,* Scarlet had repeatedly reasoned to herself, *I'll probably never see Harv again.*

*Knock. Knock.*

"Come in!"

Karyn entered Scarlet's office to drop off a new collection of articles which needed to be edited. Karyn had been cold and distant since the incident with Harv. Scarlet was more than a little curious to find out why.

"How are you?" Scarlet asked politely.

"Fine," Karyn snapped. Her eyes fell upon the recycling bin in the corner. "How long has that been full?"

"Excuse me?"

"The recycling is overflowing," Karyn noted in disgust.

"Oh, a couple of days, I guess."

Karyn shook her head disapprovingly. "That cleaning *boy* is a disgrace. I'm this close to firing him." Her index finger and thumb were almost touching, indicating the instability of Harv's job.

"I'll empty it," Scarlet hurried to say. She could easily predict what was going to happen next.

"I don't think so. That *boy* has to learn his lesson."

*What's her vendetta with Harv about?* Scarlet questioned as she watched Karyn storm off.

Instead of waiting for the inevitable to happen, Scarlet decided to take destiny into her own hands. She prepared to hurry out of her office before Harv got there.

*Crash!*

Scarlet and Harv collided into one another. She almost lost her balance, but he caught her just in time.

"Where are you going?" he inquired in a tone too serious for such a simple question.

"The bathroom."

"Stop lying to me, Scarlet."

Harv became silent as he dumped the contents of Scarlet's recycling bin into a large plastic bag.

"Stop doing this to me," Scarlet muttered more to herself than Harv.

Harv looked at Scarlet with wide eyes. "I haven't done anything." He watched as she looked at the ground. "So you feel it too." Harv stepped closer to her. "I want to know you better than I know anyone. This may seem strange because we've just met but..." Harv's voice became a whisper, "you feel it too."

"Why does Karyn hate you?" Scarlet was desperate to break the prince charming image she had created in her mind.

"I'd rather not say," Harv muttered uncomfortably.

"Then I'd rather not stay." Scarlet turned to leave.

"I rejected her indecent proposal."

"What?" Scarlet could hardly stop her mouth from falling open.

Harv stepped closer to Scarlet. "I guess Karyn is used to getting what she wants. This time she didn't."

Scarlet's heart raced with love. Harv's ideal prince charming persona had just been heavily reinforced.

"It's lunchtime. Do you want to eat outside?" Harv asked.

"Yes," Scarlet said, despite her best efforts to refuse.

It was a warm and sunny day as Scarlet and Harv sat on a bench. They had just finished their lunches and were now watching the white clouds float carelessly in the light blue sky.

"Why do you work as a cleaner?" Scarlet asked. "I can tell by the way you talk that you're an intelligent guy."

"I moved here two months ago and had no other choice. I needed the money."

"Didn't you go to school?"

"No. I'm new to this country," Harv replied.

"Where are you...?"

"Europe," he answered her unfinished question.

"Oh."

"You've done wonders for Hot Spot Magazine," Harv complimented. "With you on board, the magazine has really improved."

Scarlet smiled, happy that Harv had taken an interest in her work.

Harv suddenly leaned closer to Scarlet. More than anything, she wanted to feel her lips upon his. Instead, she pulled away.

"Not like this," Scarlet said firmly.

Harv looked distraught. "Why?"

"I have a boyfriend."

Harv was silent for a moment. "Then why does this feel so right?"

Scarlet's eyes were locked on Harv's. "I feel like I'm cheating on *you*," was all she said, before getting up and leaving.

* * *

Scarlet was grateful for the weekend. She wanted nothing more than to avoid Harv. Scarlet knew she needed to get her head straight before speaking to Harv and, especially, Trevor.

Avoiding Trevor proved to be an impossible task. She was able to avert his calls on Saturday, but on Sunday he came to her house unannounced.

*Ding Dong.*

*Go away! I'm not ready for this!* Scarlet silently screamed. She contemplated hiding behind the couch.

*Ding Dong. Ding Dong.*

Somehow, Scarlet found the strength to open the door. Standing there was Trevor; a look of concern washed over his face.

"Scarlet! Where have you been?" Trevor hugged Scarlet, making her feel extremely suffocated.

"I needed some time alone."

"But why?" Trevor looked hurt and confused.

"I feel lost and scared," Scarlet said in a voice that was hardly above a whisper.

"No, no," Trevor moaned, wrapping her in a hug again. He noted how she pulled away at his touch. "Please, Scarlet, you're killing me. What's wrong?"

"I don't know." Scarlet was now crying.

"What...what's changed?"

"Nothing." Scarlet paused slightly. "Everything."

"That doesn't make sense." He was now on the verge of tears.

"I don't love you anymore!" Scarlet cried. "Please just leave!"

"No, you can't mean it." Trevor couldn't believe what he was hearing.

"Trevor, I do."

Trevor stumbled backwards. His eyes were wide and wet as he slowly left Scarlet's house.

Scarlet sat down on her couch and sobbed.

\* \* \*

Scarlet was unsure about what she would do at work on Monday. She'd left Trevor for a man she hardly knew yet cared for deeply. Scarlet knew jumping into another relationship was a risky move for her already frazzled mental state.

As soon as Scarlet entered the hall, she saw Harv waiting outside her office door. He saw her at the same time.

"Let me speak," Harv hurried to say. "I know you have a boyfriend who must be the luckiest guy in the world. Does he realize that? Wait, I don't mean to be disrespectful. Of course you wouldn't be with a guy who didn't treat you well. How could he not? You're amazing. But I don't believe anyone could feel this way about you. I mean, of course any man would be in love with you. Just look at you – you're a dream." Harv took a deep, shaky breath. He was rambling and almost slurring upon his words. "I'll wait outside this door forever."

Scarlet let her instincts guide her as she moved closer to Harv. He followed her actions. Scarlet brought her face closer to Harv's. He met her half-way. Their eyes were closed as Scarlet and Harv's lips made contact in the most perfect way. Their first kiss was warm and soft. It lasted for several minutes, getting more passionate as the seconds passed.

After the kiss, Harv held on to Scarlet's waist, re-fusing to let her go. He pressed his face against her cheek and then kissed the soft flesh. It was essential that Harv kept his arms tight on Scarlet's waist. Otherwise, her knees would have buckled and caused her to fall to the floor.

Scarlet took a deep breath in an attempt to for-ever imprint Harv's masculine scent into her senses.

"I never want to let you go," Harv whispered into Scarlet's ear.

Scarlet's whole body was alive. "Good."

Another soft kiss on Scarlet's cheek led to their lips meeting once again.

\* \* \*

*Present Day...*

Scarlet woke up in the cabin. It took her a mo-ment to realize where she was. The rain still pounded heavily against the windows and roof.

Scarlet sat up in bed. She painfully let go of Harv's pillow. The dream had been so real; it had been an exact retelling of her reality.

"Harv?"

Silence.

*Why isn't he back yet?*

Scarlet couldn't relax enough to get back to sleep. Instead, she looked out the window. The rain was heavier than ever and the lightning flashed more frequently. Scarlet shivered. She needed Harv's arms around her.

Scarlet sat in the wicker-chair and pulled a blanket tightly around her. Her memory returned to where her dream had ended.

\* \* \*

*Late September...*

The first week Scarlet spent with Harv was pure bliss. Just being near him and touching his arms was enough to make Scarlet's heart race. She'd never felt this way about a man before. What made the experience even better was knowing that Harv felt as much love and passion as she did.

It was a rainy Saturday afternoon as Scarlet and Harv lay on the couch. The television was on but neither of them were paying attention to it. Harv's hands were gently placed on Scarlet's hips, while her hands played with his hair. Harv kissed her nose, leading to an extended make-out session.

"I love you," Harv muttered, his lips releasing Scarlet's for a mere second.

Scarlet pulled away, but only so she could place her head upon his chest. "I love you too."

Scarlet hardly felt functional. She was too in love. Scarlet listened to Harv's heartbeat until her rhythm mimicked his.

*Knock. Knock.*

"That will be Melissa," Scarlet said as she stood up. "She said she'd try to come over today."

"Ah, the best friend," Harv laughed. "I've heard a lot about her."

"And she's heard a lot about you. That's why she's here."

"To check out your goods, huh?"

"Oh yeah," Scarlet replied with a laugh. Her eyes suddenly brightened in excitement. "You answer the door. It'll totally surprise her."

*Knock. Knock.*

Harv opened the door.

Scarlet looked expectantly at the person on the other side and then cringed.

"Who the hell are you?" Trevor demanded of Harv.

"Please, don't do this," Scarlet pleaded, forecasting disaster.

"Nice, Scarlet, real nice," Trevor said, his face stone cold. He suddenly realized why she had dumped him in such a hurry.

"I'm sorry," Scarlet said.

"Didn't our love mean anything to you?" Trevor demanded.

Scarlet couldn't offer a reply.

"I'm sorry this happened, but we're in..." Harv began to say.

"Don't," Trevor interrupted. "Don't even say it." He turned to Scarlet. "You can't possibly want to be with him. I'm the guy for you, Scarlet. We're meant to be together."

"That's enough, man." Harv moved forward in an attempt to gently push Trevor out of the house.

Trevor took Harv's action as a challenge. He punched Harv in the stomach and then raced to Scarlet.

"Please, give us another chance. I love you."

"Leave." Scarlet was sympathetic but resolute.

Defeated, Trevor paused momentarily to look at Harv, who was nursing his stomach. "Sorry," he mumbled, before walking out of the house.

Scarlet comforted Harv, although he knew she was the one who needed the support and understanding.

\* \* \*

*Early February...*

With the key he had recently given her, Scarlet let herself into Harv's house on a late Sunday morning.

"Harv, are you home?" she called.

Silence.

*He must be shopping,* Scarlet rationalized. *He'll be back soon.*

Scarlet sat on Harv's couch. She was about to turn on the television when she heard a faint mutter in the background.

Curious but slightly scared, Scarlet cautiously followed the noise. The muttering became more decipherable. It sounded like someone was chanting. The noise was coming from behind the bathroom door. It was ajar, so Scarlet carefully peeked in.

Standing over the sink, Harv held something in a clear plastic bag. He continued his nonsensical chant.

Scarlet's skin tingled as she watched Harv turn on the tap. He opened the bag to reveal a small mushroom which was an odd shade of neon purple. Harv gently sprinkled water upon the mushroom and then ate it. He began to act even weirder, as if a powerful force was engulfing his body.

"Oh my gosh!" Scarlet cried as she swung the door open. "You're doing drugs?"

Harv was shocked to see Scarlet. He had calmed down and now appeared normal. "It...it's not what it seems. You don't understand."

"You're right about that. What the hell are you doing drugs for?" Scarlet snatched the bag from Harv. She looked at the small mushrooms which were various neon colors. "Damn, Harv. Did you really think you could keep this a secret?"

Harv grabbed the bag from Scarlet. "Don't touch them. They're dangerous."

"I know!" Scarlet cried furiously as she shoved Harv out of the way.

Harv gently grabbed Scarlet before she could leave. "The mushrooms are magical. They keep me alive."

"You're high."

"Look into my eyes, Scarlet. You know I'm not under any influence."

Scarlet looked into Harv's eyes. They were crystal clear and beaming with love.

"I...I don't understand."

"I think you should sit down," Harv said softly as he guided Scarlet out of the bathroom and to the living-room. He sat next to Scarlet and then began to speak. "I was born in Germany in the early nineteen hundreds."

"You said you were twenty-five," Scarlet stated, suddenly worried about Harv's mental health.

"Please, Scarlet, just listen. I was fifteen years old when I got lost in the Dark Forest for several days. I was famished until I found a stream and drank from it. Beside the stream were the craziest things I've ever seen – small neon mushrooms of every color imaginable. I was so hungry and the mushrooms were so tempting. I ate one, then two, and then three. They were so good and I felt surprisingly strong. I finally found my way home, but I came back for the mushrooms every week. Then the strangest thing happened – I stopped aging. My parents were terrified. They kept moving to hide my abnormality from society. Then, suddenly, I began to age again. It didn't take me long to realize that my aging, or rather lack of aging, had something to do with the mushrooms. I was twenty-five years old when I returned to the Dark Forest. I have been eating the special mushrooms ever since. You're the first person I've told."

Scarlet remained silent. She had no clue how to respond to what Harv had just said.

"Say something," he begged.

"Are you for real?" Scarlet finally choked out.

"Have I ever lied to you?"

"No," Scarlet admitted.

"Do you trust me?" Harv asked.

"Yes."

"Then I need your trust and belief more than ever," Harv said. "I know this sounds crazy, but it's my reality."

"How do you get the mushrooms now?"

"I have a stash, but it won't last long. I'll have to return to Germany one day soon."

Scarlet got up from the couch. Harv followed her, placing his arms around her waist. His touch felt the same as always. Nothing had changed.

"Were you ever going to tell me?" Scarlet pried.

"Yes, but how does one tell his love that he's a freak?"

"I like my men freaky," she said seductively.

Harv's whole body relaxed. "You still want to be with me?"

"Do dogs bark?" Scarlet teased.

"I love you."

* * *

*Late May...*

The stash of mushrooms soon dwindled. Harv had to return home if he was to survive. Scarlet's decision wasn't a hard one to make.

"This is it," Harv said as he opened the door to the log cabin and escorted her in. "Not a thing has changed."

Scarlet silently looked around the cabin. For an abandoned place in the middle of the Dark Forest, it was surprisingly clean and welcoming.

"Is it okay?" Harv asked anxiously.

"It'll do," Scarlet teased, before kissing Harv.

Suddenly, Harv grabbed his stomach and groaned in pain.

"What's wrong?" Scarlet panicked.

"I...I need a purple mushroom," he stuttered.

Scarlet hurried to Harv's luggage and searched through it until she found the familiar plastic bag.

Harv hardly chewed the mushroom. He needed it in him right away.

Scarlet watched in fear. *This is really happening*, she thought with a gulp.

"I have to find more mushrooms," Harv stated, after the mushroom's powers had healed him.

Scarlet nodded. It was all that she could do.

As Scarlet and Harv trekked through the Dark Forest later that day, she realized that the forest lived up to its name. The thick trees blocked most of the sunlight, making it difficult to see.

"I remember this place," Harv muttered as he led Scarlet over fallen tree limbs and around patches of large bushes. "Every inch of this place is imprinted in my mind."

"Did you always have a good memory or is it the power of the mushrooms?"

"The only thing I know is that every different mushroom has a special power. The purple ones maintain health, the yellow restore eyesight, the..." Harv stopped speaking and pulled Scarlet behind a thick tree.

"What is it?" she whispered.

Harv placed his hand over Scarlet's mouth to silence her. He was staring intensely at something she couldn't see. Harv finally let his hand fall to his side.

"Stay here," he instructed.

*He's never acted so controlling,* Scarlet thought, annoyed by his behavior.

Scarlet's eyes had now adjusted to the darkness. She was able to see the outline of trees and figures. She was especially fixated upon the man who was digging by the stream. Scarlet watched breathlessly as Harv ran to the man and grabbed him.

"Hey!" the man cried in protest.

"What are you doing here?" Harv yelled.

Silence.

Scarlet couldn't bear the tension. She ran to Harv.

"Harv?" the man asked in disbelief.

"Jeremy?" Harv choked out.

The two men looked stunned and then they hugged each other.

"I haven't seen you in decades," Jeremy began to say.

"You should be eighty by now. How did you find out?" Harv asked, cutting Jeremy off.

Scarlet peered over Harv's shoulder to see several neon mushrooms littering the ground.

Instead of replying, Jeremy hurried to collect them in a bag. He seemed possessive and obsessive.

Harv began to collect them in the same manner. Scarlet wanted to help him, but she was too scared to touch the glowing mushrooms.

Harv and Jeremy reached for the same mushroom. They looked at each other and began to fight for it.

"Stop it!" Scarlet cried as Jeremy tried to punch Harv, causing Harv to hit back. The fight continued, refusing to give heed to Scarlet's pleas.

"What are we doing?" Harv questioned after the last mushroom of the patch was securely in his hands.

"That's easy for you to say," Jeremy hissed. "Give it to me."

"I can't, but there's more," Harv replied.

"I know about patches that you couldn't even imagine."

"Your knowledge will be useless when I raid those patches." Harv was now infuriated by Jeremy's inability to accept his diplomacy.

Jeremy lunged for Harv, but Scarlet got caught in the middle. Jeremy accidentally hit her shoulder.

"Ow!" Scarlet cried out in pain.

"You bastard!" Harv seethed as he punched Jeremy's face.

Scarlet did the only thing she could – she walked away. Harv ran after her.

"Those mushrooms...they're dangerous," Scarlet gasped when Harv caught up to her.

"I've told you that since the beginning," Harv sighed. "I'll take you home, if you want."

"Let's go home." Scarlet began to lead Harv towards the cabin. He struggled to keep up since his pockets were full of mushrooms.

"Do you want help packing your bags?" Harv asked heavily as they entered the cabin.

"I'm not going anywhere," Scarlet stated.

"But you said..." Harv began to protest.

"I'm already home."

"Scarlet, if anything happens to you..."

"Then it happens. I have no regrets and neither should you."

"That may be fine for now, but we still have a problem. I'm going to stay this way forever but you...I've lost too many people, Scarlet. To lose you would kill me in a whole other sense."

"We can think about that another day," Scarlet said, touching Harv's face. "Don't tell me you don't have the time."

Despite everything, Harv laughed.

* * *

*Middle of June...*

Three weeks had passed since the incident with Jeremy. Thankfully, neither Scarlet nor Harv had heard from him. It was too painful for Harv to admit that a past friend was now a rival to his survival.
*Knock. Knock.*

"Forgot your keys again?" Scarlet joked as she put down a book and then headed towards the door. "Jeremy?" she gasped, when she saw who was standing behind the door.

"I need to speak with Harv."

"He's busy," Scarlet replied, not wanting to tell Jeremy that she was alone in the cabin.

"Whatever it is, it can't be more important than this." Jeremy's eyes looked wild, as if they were desperately hungry. "You're all alone, aren't you?"

Scarlet didn't have a chance to reply as Jeremy pushed past her and began scouring the cabin.

"Stop it! Get out!" Scarlet screamed.

Jeremy continued his search, this time heading to the bedrooms.

*He's crazy,* Scarlet thought, before running out of the cabin in search for Harv.

Scarlet looked in all the places Harv had ever taken her. Yet, she could see no sign of him. Afraid that she would become lost, Scarlet returned home.

Instead of entering her cabin, Scarlet hid behind a tree. She peered at the cabin, wondering if Jeremy was still inside. Scarlet stood out there for over an hour. Fully convinced that Jeremy had left, she entered cautiously.

The living-room was messier than usual, but everything looked calm. With a deep breath, Scarlet ascended the stairs.

The bedrooms were empty, but several drawers had been raided and left open. With a racing heart, Scarlet ran into the bathroom. She let out a small cry upon seeing the raided cabinet. All the mushrooms Harv had collected were gone.

"I can't deal with this!" Scarlet cried, before falling to the floor and weeping.

"Scarlet!" Harv ran into the bathroom and wrapped his arms around her. "I have to tell you something."

Scarlet's whole body shivered. "Please, no more."

"Scarlet, you have to know..."

"No!" Scarlet cried, pulling away from Harv and running into their bedroom. She flung herself onto the bed.

Harv lay next to Scarlet until she calmed down. "Jeremy's dead," he whispered, hugging her tightly. "I found him in the forest. I...I think he overdosed on the mushrooms." Harv had begun to choke on his words.

"How could this happen?" Scarlet whimpered as she pulled Harv even closer.

"Greed," Harv answered, contemplating his own recent behavior. "I need you with me always, Scarlet. You're the only one who keeps me sane."

Scarlet looked away from Harv's pleading eyes. She knew this day would come. "Okay."

Harv looked unconvinced at first. "You'll eat the mushrooms?"

"Yes."

"You'll live with me forever?" Harv needed to be sure Scarlet fully understood what she was getting into.

Scarlet kissed Harv passionately.

"Does that answer your question?" Scarlet asked, after their lips had finally parted.

Harv nodded, while smiling widely.

* * *

*Present Day...*

The rain continued to pour down. Loud thunder and then a nearby lightning bolt brought Scarlet back to the present moment. She sighed. The history she and Harv shared was beyond ordinary. They had been together for seventy-five years now. They were both twenty-five and more in love than ever.

*Can we really live for eternity? If all this were to end now, could I die happy?* Scarlet was unsure of how to answer her own questions.

Another lightning bolt hit the ground. The door swung open. Scarlet's head shot up to see Harv dripping wet but most definitely alive.

Scarlet ran to Harv and hugged him. "Where the hell have you been?"

"I was only half an hour longer than usual," Harv replied.

"Huh?"

"Are you alright?" he asked in concern.

Scarlet nodded, realizing that her dreams and memories had made the separation seem like days.

"I found the biggest patch ever!" Harv showed Scarlet the largest bag she'd ever seen. It was almost overflowing with mushrooms.

"This will last for years!" Scarlet said in shock.

"That's just what I intended for us."

Scarlet put the bag of mushrooms aside so she could hug Harv tightly. She didn't care that his wet clothes were dampening hers.

"You still want to live forever with me?" Scarlet muttered.

Harv pulled away so he could look into Scarlet's eyes. "More than ever. My feelings for you will never change, Scarlet – they will only increase."

Scarlet let Harv kiss her lovingly and passionately. The feeling of his strong arms around her as well as his masculine scent would forever drive her crazy.

\* \* \*

# The Truth About Fairy Tales

"He did *what?*" Destiny almost choked on her lemon iced tea. The straw she'd been sipping on fell from her mouth, rolled across the table and finally landed on the floor.

Lila looked at the straw, suddenly embarrassed that she'd spilled last night's events to Destiny. "Want me to get you a new straw?"

"Talk," Destiny demanded. "Now."

"But your straw…"

"Don't change the subject, Lila."

Lila sighed. She knew she was trapped. "Ricky told me we were going Dutch to the movies so he could buy me a great dinner. I had just bought my movie ticket when he handed the employee a buy one, get one free ticket. Needless to say, he got in for free."

"I can't believe him!" Destiny exclaimed.

"Oh, it gets worse. Much worse. At dinner he kept telling me to order anything I wanted – price was no concern. And for Ricky? He certainly spared no expense. He was chowing down on some glazed goose."

"How is this bad? Sounds to me as if he redeemed himself."

Lila ignored Destiny and continued speaking. "Ricky asked for the bill to be delivered and then he excused himself to use the bathroom. He never returned. I sat there for over half an hour. Thinking that he had fallen ill, I had an employee check the men's bathroom. Turns out Ricky escaped through a window. I had to pay for both our meals on my credit card."

Destiny's eyes were wide. Suddenly, she burst out laughing.

"Destiny! It was the worst night of my life!" Lila couldn't believe how insensitive her friend was being.

"Sorry," Destiny apologized as she attempted to muffle her laugh.

"Everything's just peach fuzz for you," Lila pouted. "Kevin's the epitome of the perfect boyfriend. You're so lucky."

Destiny's face fell. *If only you knew,* she thought.

"What about Devon?" Destiny asked quickly. She was more than a little anxious to change the subject.

"Who's that?" Lila asked, finally turning her attention to her half-melted frosty treat.

"You know him," Destiny urged. "Brown spiky hair, blue eyes...he's in our psychology class."

"Oh!" Lila suddenly remembered the hottie Destiny was referring to. "What about him?"

"I swear I've caught him looking at you."

"Why didn't you tell me this before?" Lila asked, somewhat suspiciously.

Destiny just shrugged. "I'm telling you now, aren't I? I'll talk to him. You know, give him some subtle hints that you may be interested."

"I don't know. I kind of feel like going on a guy strike."

"Don't be silly! You'll have Devon eating out of your hand by this time next week."

Lila finally laughed. "Okay. Work your magic, if you can."

"Is that a dare?" Destiny's eyes were twinkling. She loved nothing more than a challenge.

"Most certainly. Listen Dee, I have to run. Catch you in class tomorrow?"

"You know it." Destiny watched as Lila walked away. The coffee shop in the university was crowded with students, but she felt empty and lost.

Destiny loathed thinking about Kevin, yet her thoughts always returned to him. Kevin had recently admitted to cheating on her with a co-worker. Destiny was disgusted and hurt but had ultimately decided to stay with him. Kevin was Destiny's first serious boyfriend. Before him, her family and friends, with the exception of Lila, would tease her for not having a man in her life. If Destiny dumped Kevin, all those feelings of low self-worth would return. Even worse, if anyone found out that Kevin had cheated on her, they would all say it was her fault for not satisfying him in the first place.

Destiny sighed deeply. *There's something wrong with the human race when we all play roles,* she thought bitterly. *But I'm no better because I'm the phoniest of them all.*

* * *

Lila looked at herself in the mirror and smiled. She liked the fresh-faced, curly-haired girl who stared back at her. In a pink top and matching floral skirt, Lila looked pretty and respectable.

Destiny's promise to set Lila and Devon up had been fulfilled. Lila was to meet Devon at an off-campus lounge. She grabbed her bus pass from the dresser and then hurried out of the dorm. Lila was anxious but also excited to get the date started.

Lila was a bit frustrated before entering the lounge. The bus had been late and crowded. When she was inside the modern hang-out, her mood brightened. She scanned the crowd, happy at the thought of seeing Devon.

*I hope I haven't kept him waiting.*

Lila finally found the table Destiny said Devon would be sitting at. She was surprised to find it empty. Lila sat down to wait. Five minutes turned to ten and then to fifteen. Believing she had been stood up, Lila finally rose after twenty minutes of waiting.

"Hey!"

Lila twirled around to see Devon. "Hi. Is everything..."

"Were you going to leave?" Devon demanded, cutting Lila off mid-sentence.

"I..."

"You better not. I don't like to wait around for some girl."

Lila was speechless.

Devon sat down at the table and then flipped through the menu. "I'm getting a beer," he finally said. "You?"

*Just give him a chance,* Lila mentally prepared herself.

"I'm talking to you, space cadet." Devon laughed loudly.

Lila gritted her teeth. "Water."

The waitress came and Devon ordered for them. As she walked away, Lila caught Devon staring at the waitress' ass. His action was obvious and he didn't stop even when Lila cleared her throat several times.

"Miniskirts are hot," Devon observed aloud.

"Um, yeah," Lila replied awkwardly. "So, what's your major at university?"

"Law. I'm going to be a lawyer."

"Oh, you have a passion for the justice system?"

Devon snorted. "No. I just want the money."

"Oh."

The drinks came. Once again, Devon stared at the waitress' ass.

Lila and Devon remained silent as they consumed their beverages. Devon released a bored sigh every three minutes or so.

"Want to dance?" Lila tried to sound peppy.

Devon shrugged lackadaisically, but he got up anyway. She led him to the dance floor and then put her hands around his neck. Devon instantly began to dance inappropriately with her. Shocked, Lila backed away.

"What's your problem, Lily?"

"It's Lila."

"Whatever."

"You know, I'm suddenly not feeling well," Lila lied. "I really have to go home."

Devon shrugged yet again. "Later."

Lila felt like hitting Devon. Instead, she walked away.

On the bus ride home, numerous thoughts ran through Lila's head. *He didn't even offer to take me back to my dorm. I bet he's still at the lounge grinding with slutty girls. He's such a jerk.*

By the time Lila arrived back at her dorm, she was emotionally exhausted. *I can't do this anymore,* she thought as she got ready for bed. *No more idiots ever again!*

\* \* \*

As the weeks went by, Lila returned to her happy-go-lucky self. The memories of Ricky and

Devon had faded, leaving her with the desire to find a man worthy of her affection.

Lila was thankful for having her own dorm as she connected to the internet and typed "find a good man" into a search engine. The results of Lila's search shocked her. That wasn't the kind of service she was looking for. Lila changed her words to "find your true love."

*This is more like it,* she thought as she browsed through the numerous sites which hosted personals.

An hour had passed and Lila was about to turn off the computer. However, at the last second, something caught her eye. "Find Your Prince Charming," she muttered. Lila clicked on the link.

The website opened with a bang, literally. The screen was black for a mere second and then colorful fireworks exploded. When the fireworks ceased to pop, beautiful scenery of a moor and a castle appeared.

"Welcome to the life you deserve," a man's voice came over the computer. The man exited the castle and proceeded to the forefront of the screen. He was extremely handsome with thick brown hair and sparkling blue eyes. "My name is James," the man continued. "I created Find Your Prince Charming because I believe that every woman deserves to be treated like a princess. This isn't your average dating service where any man can create a profile. I know each man personally and can vouch for their superior attitude and behavior. My service is for women who are looking to meet their prince charming. Just fill in the survey and I will introduce you to your perfect match."

*Sounds a bit commercial,* Lila thought as photographs of happy couples littered the screen. *But then again, there's no gain without risk.* Lila clicked on the survey link and began filling in the answers.

*How would your ideal man behave? He would be considerate and caring and give all his attention to me.*

*What would your ideal man look like? He would be tall and well-built with blonde hair and blue eyes.*

Lila had fun filling in the survey. The questions had become extremely specific and almost nonsensical, but she didn't mind. Lila smiled after clicking the send button. She loved the feeling of taking control of her fate.

* * *

"The weather's finally getting better," Destiny noted as she and Lila strolled past the campus garden.

"Spring will do that." Lila hardly had time to finish speaking when her cell phone rang. "Hello?"

"Lila?" a husky voice replied on the other end.

"Yeah..."

"I'm Phillip, the man Find Your Prince Charming matched you with."

Lila's face reddened. It'd been two weeks since she had filled in the survey. She had almost forgotten about it. Now, hearing Phillip's voice, everything seemed so fresh and real.

"Are you still there?"

"Um yeah. How are you, Phillip?"

"I've never felt better." There was a slight pause. "I live very close to you. Would you like to meet?"

"I'd love to." Lila knew things were moving fast, but she was happy about it.

"If it's alright, I'd love to see you tomorrow."

*Wow! This guy sounds sexy and polite!* Lila thought. "That would be fine."

After ending her call with Phillip, Lila turned happily to Destiny.

"Was that a guy?" Destiny asked, appearing somewhat jealous.

"Yup!" Lila replied cheerfully. "It was my prince charming!"

* * *

Lila's heart was racing. She took a deep breath and then smoothed her denim skirt. In preparation, she smiled confidently and then entered the coffee shop. Lila scanned the crowd.

"Lila?"

Lila lost her breath. Walking towards her was a tall, well-built, blonde-haired, blue-eyed stallion. Phillip held his hand out to Lila. She took it. He smiled widely.

"I knew you were Lila. The sweet and sexy voice I heard on the phone had to belong to such a magnificent beauty."

Phillip was so sincere that Lila instantly believed his compliments.

Phillip led Lila to a table in the corner of the coffee shop. He pulled the chair out for her and then politely pushed her forward.

"Thank you." Lila was very impressed.

Phillip handed Lila a menu. "Please, order whatever you like, but may I recommend the strawberry lemonade smoothie? You seem like a lady who would enjoy such a sweet treat."

"I'd love that."

The waitress came and Phillip ordered for the both of them. He didn't acknowledge the waitress' miniskirt. In fact, he hardly took his eyes off Lila.

"You said you attended university but never mentioned your major," Phillip inquired.

"It's psychology," Lila said.

"What a wonderful field of study. I'm doing my PhD in psychology."

Lila was now extremely impressed with Phillip.

As the date continued, Phillip was attentive and caring – a perfect gentleman. The drinks, which Phillip paid for, had been finished long ago, but the date was no where near over.

"It's such a lovely night that I thought you might enjoy a cruise down the Floral Canal," Phillip suggested.

A small gasp escaped from Lila's mouth. The Floral Canal was the town's main attraction. Only two people, as well as the guide, were allowed on the boat. It was a beautiful but extremely expensive experience.

"Would you like that?" Phillip asked with a gorgeous smile.

"I've never been because of the price," Lila admitted.

"It would be worth every penny if I could see you smile." Phillip reached across the table to gently stroke Lila's cheek and chin.

Lila had to hold onto the table to avoid falling over. His hands were smooth but masculine. In Lila's opinion, Phillip was beyond swoon-worthy. "I...I'd love that so much," she finally choked out.

The scenery was serene and the atmosphere was perfect. The white boat floated gently down the Floral Canal. The flowers, which made the tour so famous, littered the edge of the canal. They stood bright and proud in the large decorative pots.

"It's getting a bit chilly," Phillip noted as he took off his jacket and offered it to Lila. She let him place it upon her shoulders. It made her feel warm and secure.

Lila looked at the water which was illuminated by the moonlight.

"You look absolutely beautiful," Phillip said, gazing into Lila's eyes. "I know we've just met, but would you mind if I...?" Phillip gently guided Lila's face towards his own. Their lips met in the most perfect kiss.

Phillip was sweet and polite, but Lila could feel the passion burning in his lips. Finally, Lila backed away just because she needed to breath.

"Your lips and kiss were wonderful," Phillip complimented.

Lila could feel the adoration Phillip had for her as he held her hand. *He's such a keeper,* she thought as she snuggled into his chest.

* * *

"It's been a month!" Lila exclaimed as she and Destiny walked to class early one morning. "A whole month of nothing but bliss!"

"Find Your Prince Charming is amazing." As soon as the words had left Destiny's mouth, she regretted them.

Lila looked suspicious. "How would you know?"

Destiny was trapped and she knew it. "I kind of checked out the website for myself."

"But why? Kevin is your perfect guy."

"No, he's not!" Destiny cried unexpectedly. Months of holding the truth in had finally caught up to her. "He cheated on me, Lila. He's a good-for-nothing jerk!"

Lila's eyes grew wide. "What? When did this happen?"

"Two months ago."

"Oh, Destiny." Lila hugged her friend. "Why didn't you tell me sooner?"

"I was embarrassed and thought it was my fault."

"Oh, Destiny."

"Stop saying that! I'm not stupid, you know. I've dumped Kevin and never want to see him again."

Lila sighed with relief. "Good. So, what made you change your mind?"

"Christopher," Destiny stated simply.

"Christopher?"

"My very own prince charming."

Lila squealed and then hugged Destiny once again. "Where do they find such amazing guys?" she wondered out loud.

* * *

All eyes were on Lila and Destiny as they entered the dance. It was the Spring Fling, the biggest and best social which was second only to the end-of-the-year formal. Phillip and Christopher were at their sides. The two couples looked like royalty, as if they had just stepped out of a fairy tale.

Phillip and Christopher escorted their dates to the reserved table and, of course, offered them chairs. Lila and Destiny sat down, loving the fact that all their fellow female students were as jealous as hell.

A light meal was being distributed. Phillip and Christopher ate with grace, while most of the male students ate with their fingers when they should have been using a fork.

After the meal was finished and there had been half an hour of entertaining yet polite conversation, the lights dimmed and music began to play.

"May I have this dance?" Phillip and Christopher asked simultaneously as they held their hands out to Lila and Destiny.

Lila and Destiny were led to the dance floor where they were twirled and almost swept off their feet. Once again, all eyes were on the too-good-to-be-true couples.

"Hi sexy," the university's most promiscuous girl cooed at Phillip.

Phillip motioned towards Lila. "She must be talking to you, sexy."

The promiscuous girl looked beaten but not down. "How about a dance?"

"No, thank you." Phillip held Lila tightly, while gazing into her eyes.

Defeated and in a huff, the girl stormed away.

*Phillip's everything I've ever wanted in a man,* Lila thought as he kissed her gently but passionately.

"FBI! Everybody freeze!" someone suddenly shouted.

Students screamed and proceeded to do everything but freeze. As Lila's eyes flew open, she saw students running for cover in the bathroom and under tables. Some were even trying to escape through windows.

"I said freeze!"

The music ceased and all the students became still. Even the Spring Fling coordinators looked shocked and terrified.

Destiny cast Lila a surprised look. Lila held Phillip tighter; it was the only thing that could offer her some comfort.

"It's going to be alright, my love," Phillip whispered into Lila's ear.

The two FBI agents walked further into the gymnasium, wearing stone cold expressions.

Lila noticed that both of the agents held strange-looking devices. She prayed that it wasn't some sort of gun.

The agents appeared to be having a serious conversation while keeping their eyes on the crowd. At the same time, they pressed a button on the hand-held devices. A low hum, hardly audible to the human ear, sounded.

"What are they doing?" Destiny muttered.

"Ow!" Phillip moaned, before falling to the floor.

"Ah!" Christopher cried as he slumped over.

Terrified, Lila and Destiny comforted their men.

"What's wrong with them?" Lila cried.

"I don't know!" Destiny was almost in tears.

*Thud. Thud.* Pounding footsteps could be heard. Lila and Destiny both looked up to see the FBI agents running towards them. The closer the agents got, the more painful Phillip and Christopher's cries became.

"That must be them!" one of the agents yelled.

The two agents grabbed Phillip and Christopher who, in their current state, were no match for the trained professionals.

"Please, stop it!" Lila begged.

"We were just dancing!" Destiny protested as the agents began to drag Phillip and Christopher across the gymnasium.

"A lot more than dancing has been going on," one of the FBI agents replied, obviously softened by the girl's pitiful cries. He turned off the device, which now in his pocket. The hum ceased to sound. Phillip and Christopher slowly began to recover.

The agents nodded to each other and then proceeded to handcuff Phillip and Christopher. Still weak and astonishingly not that shocked, Phillip and Christopher allowed themselves to be taken away.

"I'll see you soon, my love!" Phillip and Christopher simultaneously called to Lila and Destiny.

Lila and Destiny were in shock. All the students looked at them, bewildered at what they had just seen. Suddenly, Lila grabbed Destiny's hand.

"We need to know what's going on," Lila stated.

Phillip, Christopher and the two FBI agents had just exited the gymnasium. Lila pulled Destiny through the gym doors and then encouraged her to kneel behind a large garbage container. They watched silently as Phillip, Christopher and the agents drove away in a long black car.

"Come on!" Lila grabbed a bike that lay against the university and then sat on it.

"You can't steal someone's bike!" Destiny protested.

Lila rolled her eyes. "I'll return it."

Doubtfully, Destiny positioned herself on the handlebars. Lila began to pedal furiously. She was determined to follow the car and get her man back.

Sweat dripped down Lila's forehead and her breath came out in shallow rasps. She'd been racing on the bike for half an hour.

"Let me pedal," Destiny offered.

Lila refused. She pushed herself even harder as the large black car turned down an unfamiliar road.

"Where are they going?" Lila muttered, more to herself than Destiny.

"This is a bad part of town," Destiny warned.

"Shhh!"

The black car came to an abrupt stop outside a low-rise building.

"Something's not right here," Lila muttered.

"You just figured that out now?"

"Dee, no FBI agent would work from a location like this. These guys can't be legit."

The two FBI agents exited the car and then dragged Phillip and Christopher out. They didn't resist the agents. In fact, Phillip and Christopher looked like dummies, as if they relied on the agents to hold them up.

The agents carried Phillip and Christopher into the building. The sound of the door slamming shut echoed throughout the street.

"What do they want with Phillip and Christopher?" Destiny asked anxiously.

"We're about to find out."

Lila and Destiny left the bike at the side of the road and then crept towards the building.

"It'll be locked," Destiny worried out loud.

Lila tried the door. It opened. They hurried into the building. It was dark inside. The only light came from a few stray light bulbs.

Suddenly, footsteps sounded nearby. Both girls stopped dead in their tracks. Finally, the footsteps grew faint.

"No guy, not even Christopher, is worth this. I'm out of here."

"Destiny!"

Destiny didn't reply. She was too preoccupied with leaving.

"I'll never leave you, Phillip," Lila whispered as she moved forward.

Lila tried to follow the echoing footsteps, but that soon became impossible to navigate by. It sounded as if the footsteps were coming from every direction.

*Now what?* Lila thought.

Lila saw something shiny on the ceiling. A flickering light bulb revealed an air vent. Lila followed the vent, hoping that it would lead her to something, anything.

"How should we transport them?" Lila faintly heard an agent ask. She'd come to a door that was slightly ajar; a low glow was seeping through it.

"Take them and run," the agent replied with a laugh.

"Shut up."

Lila peeked through the door. She saw Phillip and Christopher lying lifelessly on the floor. She gasped loudly.

The two agents looked in Lila's direction. She ducked behind the door just in time.

"Did you hear something?" an agent asked.

Lila didn't hear the other agent's reply. Instead, she heard approaching footsteps. *Not again,* she prayed as she slid into the darkness.

The FBI agents were only a few feet away from Lila.

"Someone's here," an agent warned.

"I see something," he agreed.

Lila held her breath. Suddenly, the agents ran away from her and down the hall.

Curious, Lila stepped forward. In the distance she saw the flickering light bulb. *That's probably what he saw,* Lila thought. Realizing that time wasn't on her side, she ran into the room.

"Phillip?" Lila whispered in pain as she knelt beside him. He was so still that she thought he was dead. However, placing her head upon his chest revealed that Phillip was very much alive.

"Wake up," Lila moaned as she harshly shook Phillip. Running her hand over his chest, she began to cry.

"What the hell?" Lila was terribly startled when her index finger fell into Phillip's bellybutton. With a lump in her throat, Lila lifted Phillip's shirt. She looked at where his bellybutton should be and then screamed. Lila's eyes were met with a large gaping hole. The hole plunged deep into Phillip's stomach, yet there was no blood or any other signs of distress.

"Phillip?" Lila no longer knew who she was talking to.

"Hey!" an agent called.

Lila jumped at the sound of the voice. She prepared to run.

"Stop!"

Lila stopped. She knew she was trapped. One of the so-called FBI agents was blocking her only path to freedom.

"What...what have you done to Phillip and Christopher?" Lila stuttered.

"Is that what they're called?" the agent asked.

Lila remained silent. She became tense as he approached her.

"I'm sorry you've been fooled, but Phillip and Christopher aren't real." When Lila refused to talk, the agent continued. "They're human-structured robotics covered in a synthetic material."

"No! I've felt his breath, his heart!" Lila cried.

"That's the added features to increase believability."

"Shut up!" the other FBI agent yelled at his partner as he charged into the room. "What the hell is your problem?" The agent turned to face Lila and then grabbed her. "She can't know anything about this."

"She's already involved...with the *creation*." The agent looked disgusted. "She needed to know."

"You're going to get us killed."

Lila struggled in the agent's grasp, but he refused to let her go.

"Stay still," he commanded Lila.

"Let her go," the more sensible agent ordered.

"She's coming with us."

"Just leave her alone. We're not getting paid enough to..."

"Shut up!"

"Why don't you shut up? I'm getting really sick of you."

"Maybe Droid should have made this a one man operation," the agent holding Lila snapped.

The agent, who was the lesser of the two evils, punched the other agent's face. Lila was released from the strong grasp.

Lila hurried to Phillip's side, adamant that she could do something to help him. However, he lay deadly still and she had no idea how to aid him.

The agent who had been hit retaliated, punching so hard that the other agent fell to the ground. "This partnership is over!" he yelled.

"It was over a long time ago. All of this is over." The agent was on the floor, bleeding from his lip.

"Droid will deal with you and her." The agent left, slamming the door behind him.

The bleeding agent hurried to his feet.

"Wait!" Lila cried.

He stopped briefly. Sighing, he dug into his suit pocket to reveal a CD. He gave it to Lila and prepared to leave.

"Wait!" Lila was exasperated. "What about Phillip and Christopher?"

"It's best to leave them here. The CD holds the answers you're looking for."

Lila was now alone in the room. Torn, she left Phillip and Christopher.

Outside, the bike was gone.

*I can't believe Destiny left me,* Lila thought.

"Pssst...Lila!" Destiny peeked from the side of the building. "One man left in the car, the other ran away shortly after. What happened in there?"

Lila stared angrily at Destiny and then sat on the bike which had been discreetly moved.

"Talk to me," Destiny begged as she refused to sit on the bike's handlebars.

"Get on."

Destiny finally listened to Lila's instructions.

Back at Lila's dorm, she put the CD into her computer. She'd dropped Destiny off at her own dorm. Although she would forgive her someday, right now Lila refused to answer any of Destiny's questions. She knew this would be too much for her friend to handle.

"Welcome to Project Droid," a man spoke.

*Droid?* Lila remembered the agent mentioning that name.

"Project Droid was created with the intent of experimenting with human-like robotics for use in warfare. However, it has recently come to my attention that an employee has been harvesting our creations and selling them to entrepreneurs for undesignated purposes. The creations must be found immediately."

Lila gasped when she saw a gorgeous half-naked man lying on the table. She shivered. It reminded her of Phillip.

"To deactivate, please remove the plastic cylinder located in the bellybutton."

Lila felt like being sick as she saw the man remove the cylinder.

"This will render the creation useless until reinserted."

To Lila's surprise, the CD stopped. She restarted the computer, thinking that it may have crashed. However, upon listening to the CD again, Lila knew she had heard all the information it offered.

An hour later, Lila was racing back to the abandoned building. She had to get to Phillip and Christopher before Droid or his workers did.

Lila ran into the familiar building and through its hallway. She stopped outside the room which contained the handsome experiments; someone was already in there.

Lila watched silently as the bad agent and another man examined the room.

"I tried to constrain him, Droid, but he got away."

"If the others can't find him, we'll have to move our operations elsewhere," Droid stated.

Due to the fact that Phillip and Christopher were still lying lifelessly on the floor, Lila knew they were talking about the agent who had given her the CD.

"What about these creations?"

"They've already been shaped by external socialization," Droid replied in disgust. "They're useless. Destroy them."

Lila hid as Droid and the agent exited the room. When it was safe to do so, Lila hurried into the room and began to drag Phillip and Christopher. She held each man's hand tightly, straining herself in the process.

"Well, what do we have here?"

Lila's blood went cold. The agent stared at her, slightly amused and extremely cocky.

"Please, no one needs to know about Project Droid," Lila begged. "Just let me reactivate Phillip and Christopher."

The agent suddenly turned angry. "That idiot told you everything."

"Yes." Thinking quickly, Lila added, "He even told me what *you* did."

The agent began to lose his confidence. "I don't know what you're talking about."

"Sure you do. I doubt Droid would be very happy to hear about your misconduct."

The agent looked pale with fear. "What do you want?"

"The cylinders. I don't care about your project. I just want Phillip and Christopher to myself."

The agent looked trapped. Finally, he dug into his pocket to retrieve the two cylinders. He handed them to Lila. She reached for them, but he pulled back at the last second. "These are for your silence."

"I understand."

The agent gave Lila the cylinders. "I have to burn this place."

Lila nodded. "That's the only way to keep *our* secret."

The agent helped Lila take Phillip and Christopher out the back door. He said nothing as he returned inside. Lila couldn't believe that her ambiguous but completely made-up threat had worked.

Outside, Lila placed the cylinder in Christopher's bellybutton. His eyes shot open and then he stood up.

"Where have I been?" Christopher asked.

"It's a long story." Lila turned to Phillip. Taking a deep breath, she placed the cylinder inside him.

Phillip looked up at Lila with wide eyes. He grabbed her in an embrace. "I'm alive! Thank you! Thank you so much!"

"You're welcome."

"I'll never leave you, Lila," Phillip promised. "I'll treat you like a princess."

"No," Lila said bluntly.

"No?" Phillip looked very confused. "But you saved Christopher and I. You must want us to be a prince charming for you and Destiny."

"You can feel, Phillip, so I know it's right that you live. But your feelings for me...they're what you were trained to do. They aren't real."

Phillip looked saddened. "Then I have failed."

"No," Lila disagreed.

"No?"

Lila laughed. "Relax, Phillip. You don't have to be anyone but your synthetic self."

Phillip smiled, but it faded quickly. "Where do I go from here?"

"This time the decision is totally up to you."

Phillip walked to Christopher, who was waiting anxiously for him. He turned around one last time. "Goodbye, Lila."

"Goodbye, Phillip."

Lila watched as Phillip and Christopher walked away. She knew they would be alright because they had each other.

For the longest time, Lila had believed that love was about finding the perfect guy and being swept off her feet. Now, after everything she had been through, Lila believed that compassion was the foundation of true love.

* * *

# *Lure Of The Merman*

Bree had gone from jogging to running in a matter of minutes; that's how quick the storm had started. One minute she had been trotting barefoot through the sand and monitoring her heart rate. Then the next minute she was being hit with large raindrops. Grey clouds had rolled in fast, leaving the mid-afternoon day looking like dusk. A flash of lightning illuminated the beach. The crash of thunder sounded soon after.

Her heart monitor began to beep. Used for recreational purposes, the beeping cautioned her to slow down. However, Bree had no intention of reducing her speed. For someone who was an outdoor enthusiast, she hated to admit that lightning and thunder terrified her.

"Oh, hell no!" Bree cursed as she came to an abrupt stop. She'd jogged further today than usual and, at the time, hadn't reasoned that she'd need to once again pass the rocks which protruded onto the beach. The tide had come in, leaving Bree stranded.

The rain was still pouring down, but at least the lightning had momentarily stopped. Bree looked up at the rocks. They were steep and slippery but also pitted. Taking a deep breath and ignoring the rumbling in the sky, Bree began to scale the rocks.

Bree was only a few feet off the ground when her left foot slipped. Her leg scraped against the rock, causing pain to shoot throughout her body. Bree tried to continue climbing but it was no use. Her arms and legs ached even before she crashed onto the sandy ground.

She felt like crying as she struggled to stand up. Her leg was bleeding and the cold raindrops were decreasing her temperature rapidly. Bree thought the best thing to do was take shelter against the rock. She pressed her back against the hard stone, continually moving to find the most sheltered area. Suddenly, Bree fell backwards. In the darkness that surrounded her, she felt herself falling.

Bree landed with a thud on a soft sandy floor and then she began to sink.

*Quicksand!* Bree panicked, while struggling to fight against the downward pull.

"Let yourself go," an enchanting male voice echoed in Bree's ears.

Bree listened to the voice. Her body sank deeper but stopped when the sand had reached her knees.

"See, you're alright."

"Who's there?" Bree demanded.

"I'm the wave that pushes you forward when the current tries to bring you down."

"Huh?"

"I'm the whisper you hear in the seashell," the ethereal voice spoke again.

"Who?"

"Do you trust me?" the voice without a body asked.

"Not particularly." Bree was simultaneously excited and scared by the mysterious voice.

The man laughed. "Then I dare you to step forward."

"Okay." Bree pulled her legs out of the sand and proceeded forward. It was pleasantly hot and the air overwhelmingly smelled like saltwater. Bree felt a weird sense of comfort overcome her.

A shimmering blue light appeared like an orb in the distance. Mesmerized, Bree walked towards it. The glittering light grew stronger and more magnificent.

"Watch your step!" the voice suddenly warned.

Bree plunged into the water with a loud splash. Underneath, her eyes were open and experiencing the scene with no difficulty. Schools of brightly colored fish were swimming nearby. Bree reached towards them, but they swam away. Even the floor was covered with seashells which were a vast array of colors. Bree was about to pick up a starfish when her lungs began to ache.

Swimming to the surface, Bree gasped for air. Breathing slowly, she took in the scene around her. She was in a round enclosure. The walls seemed to dance as the underwater light flickered with the lapping water.

Bree swam as quickly as she could to the wall. Something had caught her attention. She ran her fingers over the carvings. From Bree's estimation, they were ancient drawings which probably held great meaning to the natives who had created them. She saw carvings which seemed to honor fish, shells, dolphins and seahorses, and others which discredited sharks and jellyfish. Diagrams following the changes in weather and water patterns were also displayed.

Although the scenery was beautiful and almost magical, Bree was suddenly concerned. She could see a large hole overhead.

*I must have fallen through there,* Bree reasoned. *How the hell am I going to get out?* She knew climbing out wasn't an option.

"Help me! I'm trapped!" Bree suddenly cried.

Bree's heart started to beat rapidly as waves rocked her back and forth. Something was approaching her from under the water. She was trapped. There was no sandy beach or any way to exit the water. She pressed her body against the rocky wall and then let out a blood-curdling scream.

A man emerged half way out of the water. He took one look at Bree's terrified face and then gently stroked her blonde hair.

"Please don't be afraid," he said.

Bree screamed in the man's face, causing him to cover his ears and back away. The man appeared to be resting without treading water. Bree, on the other hand, was exhausted by her efforts to stay afloat.

"I'm so sorry," the man apologized. "I wouldn't have brought you here if I knew how scared you would be."

Bree stared at the man with wide eyes. He had blonde hair and blue eyes. He also had strong features and a muscular upper body.

"You...you brought me here?" Bree finally stuttered.

The man nodded and moved closer to Bree. She couldn't stay afloat any longer, so she allowed herself to be supported by his arm. Bree felt a fish touch and then swim past her feet. However, she was so tired that she didn't bother to look down.

"I've been watching you for weeks," he said.

"I just moved here two months ago."

"I thought as much."

There was a lump in Bree's throat as she asked, "Are you going to hurt me?"

"Of course not!" the man exclaimed, his own eyes now wide. "I admire your beauty and just want to talk to you."

There was so much sincerity in the man's voice that, against her better judgment, Bree believed him.

"What are you doing down here?" Bree asked. "You shouldn't be swimming in such a storm."

"What storm?" he asked with a smile.

There was a moment of silence as Bree listened. The storm had stopped, or if it hadn't, she couldn't hear or feel its fury.

"Who are you and what are you doing here?" Bree demanded.

"I'm the breeze in your hair as you lie on the beach. The sun..."

"Stop!" Bree freed herself from the man's grasp, which he easily allowed.

"I just wanted to meet you. I'm Sandy."

Bree snorted but shook the hand Sandy offered her. "I'm Bree. Listen, you seem like a nice guy. Now that we've met, can you show me how to get out of here?"

Sandy's face fell in disappointment. "If that's what you really want, then take my hand."

Bree did as she was told. The next thing she knew, she was under the crystal clear water.

Bree had been underwater for several minutes. The time had just flown by. There was so many fish and shells to see as she and Sandy swam.

From the side of Bree's eye, she saw a large fish following them. She gasped and swam quicker, but it continued to stalk them.

Suddenly, a new fear entered Bree's mind – she was breathing underwater! In a panic, she broke to the surface.

"What's the matter?" Sandy asked.

"I...I could breath down there. How long were we under?"

"Around ten minutes."

Bree and Sandy had traveled quite a distance. The water was darker and choppier.

"That's not possible," Bree protested.

Sandy smiled widely. "Believe, Bree, and never deny anything."

"I just want to go home."

Still in the cavern, Bree and Sandy swam near the top of the water. They dived through a hole and resurfaced in the open sea.

The sky was clear and the bright sun was just beginning to set.

"Aren't you coming out?" Bree asked when Sandy failed to follow her onto the shore.

Sandy shook his head. "The water is where I'm meant to be."

"I really think you should come in. What if the weather changes again?"

"Don't you get it? *I* made the storm so we could meet." Sandy was smiling in an odd manner.

"Alright, Sandy. You take care." Bree hurried along the beach, desperate to get away from her new acquaintance.


"Where the hell were you?" Luke demanded as Bree entered their sea view house. "You were gone forever and when that storm hit, I was worried sick."

"Thanks for the concern, but I'm fine."

"You don't look fine." Luke studied Bree's damp clothing and hair.

"I can take care of myself," Bree informed Luke, before entering the bathroom.

*He can be so overbearing,* Bree thought as she slipped out of her cold clothing and into a warm bath.

96

As she lay there, an idea formed in her mind. *What if I really can breathe underwater?* Bree looked at the digital clock on the counter which read 7:48. She then dunked her head under the water. Bree's mouth was tightly shut at first. Finally, she let her face relax. To Bree's astonishment, no water encroached in her mouth or up her nose. She also realized that her vision was perfect. She didn't see the blurriness that one looking underwater would usually witness. When Bree lifted her head out of the water, she looked anxiously at the clock. It read 8:01.

Bree was both nervous and excited. Something had happened in that underwater cavern; something that was special but also supernatural.

Bree's sleep was filled with nightmares. She dreamt that she was choking on air and was only able to live under the sea. Bree could never see her family or friends again. Her only companion was Sandy.

"Sandy!" Bree woke up in a sweat. He had been so alive and close in her dreams.

Wide awake, Bree lay in her bed for over an hour. Finally, she stood up and looked out the window. A breeze seeped through the screen, allowing Bree's long hair to swirl around her shoulders.

The scenery from Bree and Luke's house was beautiful. The sea shimmered in the distance. The gentle waves were illuminated by the lighthouse's beam which continually scanned the water. The air smelled salty and cool. Bree took a deep breath, glad that she could still inhale oxygen.

As Bree looked out at the sea, something caught her eye. It appeared as if someone was swimming in the sea. She waited impatiently for the lighthouse to cast its beam on the location once again. When the light finally hit, Bree confirmed her suspicion. There was indeed a man in the sea. The next time the light hit the man, Bree saw a large fishtail follow him as he dove down. She gasped and backed away from the window.

*What the hell is going on here?* Bree wondered with a shiver.

\* \* \*

"Bree, wake up!" Luke shouted.

"What's your problem?" Bree snapped as she was awakened by excessive shaking courtesy of Luke. Since it had taken her hours to get back to sleep, she hadn't planned on getting up any time before 9:00.

"You have to see this," Luke said, while pulling Bree out of the house and onto the beach.

Bree let out a gasp upon seeing the thing which had excited Luke. She crept towards it, anxious to get a better look. A large magnificent shell, full of twists and colors, shone brightly in the morning sun.

"If you think that's weird..." Luke let his voice trail off.

Beside the shell was a heart drawn into the sand. The words "for Bree" were also inscribed.

"Looks like someone has a secret admirer," Luke tittered.

"Jealous?"

"More like concerned. Have you met any guys?" Luke had suddenly turned serious.

"No," Bree lied.

There was a moment of silence.

"So, the shell's pretty nice. You want to keep it?"

"Shut up, Luke." Bree walked back to the house.

"What did I say?" Luke tried to lift the shell, but it was way too heavy. "Damn, some dude has it bad for Bree," he muttered to himself.

It was late in the afternoon before Bree was able to get out of the house. She'd been busy unpacking a delayed delivery, while Luke preoccupied himself with teasing her. Now that Luke had gone out to buy groceries, Bree was free to do whatever she pleased. However, she only had one thing in mind and that was to find Sandy.

Bree ran along the beach and was glad to see that there was still time to get around the protruding cliff. She hurried into the opening and then fell twice.

It didn't take long for Bree's eyes to adjust to the brightness and when they did, she realized that she was in a different part of the cavern. The walls were still covered in carvings, but these ones depicted a much more interesting scene. There was a man emerging from a shell. In the next drawing, fully emerged, it was clear that the man wasn't an ordinary human; he had a large fishtail where his legs should have been. There were several more drawings, but Bree was distracted when she felt the familiar lapping of water. She held her breath until Sandy appeared.

"I knew you would come back," he teased.

"I'm looking for answers..."

"Aren't we all?" Sandy wasn't as kind as he had been yesterday.

"I saw something last night," Bree began. "It was a merman in the sea."

Sandy's eyes widened. "You've seen them too?"

"Are you a merman?" Bree demanded.

Sandy laughed. "What?"

"You seem to live in the water..." Bree let her voice trail off. She secretly hoped he was a merman. That way, he could tell her why she could breath and see perfectly underwater.

"I love swimming, but I assure you that I live on land."

Bree quickly dove underwater and looked at Sandy's lower half. She blushed when she saw a pair of normal-looking legs.

Sandy was still laughing when Bree resurfaced. "Were you expecting a tail?"

"I...I didn't know what to expect."

"Listen," Sandy became serious, "I do believe in mermaids and mermen. That's why I spend so much time in the water. Surely you've seen the carvings. There are more of them – a lot more. And from what I've gathered, they're evil."

"Evil?" Bree suddenly felt suspicious.

"Yes. The mermaids and mermen are planning to reclaim this sea by destroying any human who enters it."

"We have to get out of here!" Bree began to panic.

Sandy stopped Bree before she could swim towards the exit. "It's dangerous to go back into the sea. Their heinous plan has begun."

"How do you know so much?" Bree asked.

"I listen to them. You must stay here while I fight the merpeople." Sandy kissed Bree's cheek and then put on a brave face. "Be strong for me."

Sandy dove under the water and through the exit. He would be in the open sea by now, and at the mercy of the mermaids and mermen.

Bree planned on waiting in that watery cavern for as long as it took. *Better safe than sorry,* she reasoned.

She had been waiting for almost two hours now. Her skin was wrinkled and her arms hurt as she used the rocky wall to support herself.

"Sandy!" Bree called, desperate to find out what was going on. She received no reply.

Unable to take the suspense, Bree dove underwater and into the sea. She proceeded cautiously through the water, looking around herself in case an angry merperson was about to attack. Yet, Bree saw nothing but a calm sea. There were two adults swimming, a few teenagers lounging on a float and even children building a sandcastle at the edge of the water.

Bree swam to shore, unhappy and confused. She stumbled onto the beach, suddenly feeling unwell. It felt as if the sun was burning her eyes and skin. Even walking on the sand proved difficult; her legs had become like sticks, unable to bend or move properly.

Bree was terrified but she was even more shocked to see Sandy lying carelessly on the beach. She stumbled towards him, causing people to stare at her with concern.

"Sandy!" Bree was surprised by her voice. It sounded hoarse and felt completely dry.

Sandy opened one eye. Bree could tell that he was trying to maintain a cool exterior. "Do I know you?"

"You lunatic!" Bree lunged towards Sandy. "Whoa!" She lost her balance and fell to the sand. Her whole body ached and burned. "What's happening to me?" Suddenly, Bree's legs felt as if they were melting.

Loud screams could be heard all over the beach.

"What...what is *it*?" Sandy cried in terror.

The crazy sensations began to subside. Bree squinted and was able to see that a crowd had formed a circle around her. Every single person had a look of horror upon their faces as they stared at her legs.

"My legs!" Bree had a horrible hunch about what was happening. She looked down at herself and then screamed. There, were her legs should have been, was a colorful blue and purple mermaid tail.

Bree flapped against the sand, desperate to get back into the sea.

"Somebody catch it!" Sandy yelled.

Sandy, along with two other people, reached for Bree. She shot them down by flicking her tail excessively.

As if by some weird instinctive reaction, Bree let out a shrill cry. All the people on the beach, with the exception of Sandy, covered their ears and looked as if they were in pain.

Bree crawled and flapped her way to the sea. Sandy ran after her, but he was too late. Right before Bree swam into the sea, she saw Sandy's face. He wore a strange expression of triumph.

Bree felt alive as she swam through the sea. She was surprised by how easy it was to travel long distances in a short period of time.

After hours of aimless swimming, Bree retreated to the cavern. She could now navigate anywhere in the sea with no difficulty. This should have startled Bree but it didn't. After the day she'd had, nothing could surprise her.

The cavern seemed more comfortable than ever. It was scary how fast she was getting used to living underwater. Bree was saddened by the thought of never returning to her normal self.

*Will I ever see Luke again? What will he do without me?* Bree began to cry. Her teardrops hit the water with a deafening splash.

Bree was beginning to get tired. She leaned against the wall, preparing for sleep. The carvings scraped her skin. Bree cursed silently and then looked at the drawings. She let out a small gasp. Bree could now read the inscriptions.

She ran her hand over the carvings which showed a merman emerging from a shell. It told the story of the merpeople's creation. Their existence had started after the ice age. Large shells had been frozen at the bottom of the sea. Inside each shell was a mermaid or merman. They thawed and then crawled out of their shells. Through echolocation they found one another and started an underwater community.

Bree felt sick. The shell that was left on the beach for her was Sandy's birth shell. It wasn't a gift but a mean joke that told of his evil plan.

The next set of carvings was much less awe-inspiring. They told the story of how the merperson race thrived until the late thirteenth century. At that time, sea exploration had brought stress, capture and environmental degradation to the mermaids and mermen.

Bree was intrigued by all the stories, but it was the carvings that lay deep in the cavern's walls which frightened her. The drawings described how the merpeople were being caught and then labeled as freaks. Even more degrading was having their exis-tence denied and merely shrugged off as being a myth. This instilled a self-hatred in the underwater creatures. A "cure" to the merperson's complex was greatly sought after. Finally, one mermaid found the answer. The only way to get rid of one's tail was to switch places with a human.

Bree cried out in fury. Sandy had tricked and betrayed her. She was now and forever a mermaid. She began to sob once again.

"I heard your tears and wanted to know if you're alright."

Bree looked up upon hearing the kind voice. She saw a brown-haired, blue-eyed man. "Are...are you one of them?" she stuttered.

In response, the man flicked his green tail out of the water.

"I'll take that as a yes," Bree mumbled.

"Who are you?" the merman asked. "I've never seen you before."

"I'm not really a mermaid. Sandy took the human out of me."

The merman's mouth fell open. "That Sandy is one bad urchin."

"You know him?"

He nodded. "I'm Blue. I used to go to school with Sandy."

"You have education down here?" Bree was flabbergasted.

"Yes, but from what I've heard, it's very different than the school humans go to. Tell me, what's it really like up there?"

"I'll tell you whatever you want, but please help me first," Bree begged.

Blue frowned. "I'm not sure I can. Sandy must have lured you here and then began the transference."

"The transference?"

"You've changed places with Sandy. He has your legs and you have his tail. That's what happens when a human enters the sacred caverns."

"Can it be reversed?" Bree begged for a solution.

"I don't have the answers you're looking for."

"Then take me to someone who can."

Blue nodded. "If that's what you want, but I must warn you…"

"Just take me!"

Frightened, Blue was silent as he led Bree out of the cavern and through the water.

Bree was tense as they swam, even though she felt as if she was one with the sea. School of fish followed her as if she was their leader and a dolphin spoke to her via echolocation. The kind dolphin had complimented Bree on her pretty, shiny tail.

Blue suddenly came to a stop. "I will not go any further."

"Why not?"

"I'm too…"

"Oh, whatever!" Bree interrupted. "Where do I go from here?"

"Straight ahead. You'll soon come to a large chasm – go down there."

Bree took off swimming.

"Wait!" Blue cried.

Bree ignored his cry as she swam in a straight line. The water had become darker and deeper. She hesitated at the chasm. It looked like an endless abyss.

Suddenly, Bree felt something nudge her from behind. Certain that it was the friendly dolphin, she turned around. Bree let out a horrified scream. She was face-to-face with a deadly-looking shark. With no other reasonable choice at hand, Bree dove into the chasm. The water had turned ice-cold, but she didn't have time to worry about that. The shark was close behind her.

Bree saw a clump of seaweed swaying back and forth. She hurried into it but was repulsed by how slimy it felt. The seaweed seemed to grab at her, as if they had a mind of their own.

*Oh no!* Bree's whole body froze in fear. She was caught in the seaweed and the shark was now circling her. Bree struggled to free herself, but she was too tangled.

"Away!" a larger-than-life voice boomed. Bree stayed still, but the shark immediately turned and swam away upon hearing the voice.

Bree watched in amazement as a beautiful woman emerged from the sea's floor. She was a mermaid, but there was something intrinsically different about her. The woman wore a crown on her head and held a golden spear. Bree immediately knew this was the woman who could help her.

"Please, I need to..." Bree began to say.

"I know," the woman interrupted. "I am Crystal Waters. I see everything."

"Are you a queen?" Bree felt somewhat dumbfounded.

Crystal Waters nodded sadly. She summoned to the ground, causing a throne to appear. She sat on it, clearly disturbed. "I am the queen."

"Then why didn't you stop Sandy from doing this to me? Why didn't you destroy that cavern?"

"That cavern is sacred!" Crystal Waters snapped.

"Sorry." In her anger, Bree had been humbled. "Please, help me."

"It's too late."

"No! Why?" Bree begged.

"It's too late for me to help you. My powers have been usurped by my horrid husband. He has cast me into this dark chasm just to spite me."

"Bad marriage, huh?"

Crystal Waters rose from her throne. Bree could see the queen's sad eyes as she came closer. "I will help you, but only if you help me."

"I will, if I can."

"The sea is still your oyster – you can travel wherever you please. I need you to go to King Octopus' castle and steal back the diamond heart."

Bree sighed deeply. "How will I ever get it?"

Crystal Waters put her hands on Bree's shoulders and studied her carefully. "Be a siren, my dear. Lure the diamond heart to you!"

Bree could hardly breathe. She was outside King Octopus' castle, preparing herself for either freedom or demise. She had been there for almost half an hour, studying the guards and waiting for an opportunity to sneak by. Unfortunately, the guards had remained steadfast.

She took a deep breath and then she began to sing. Her vocals were perfect with just the right amount of mysteriousness and sexiness. The two guards looked up instantly. Bree sang for a little while longer, causing the guards to become disoriented. Finally, she revealed herself.

Bree could tell from the looks on the guards' faces that they were mesmerized by her. She sang louder than before. More mermen swam out of the castle.

"My mermen," Bree began once all the guards were surrounding her with love-stricken gazes, "I am looking for a husband." She waited until the cheers died down. "To win my love you must fight like a true merman."

Bree pointed to random guards, pairing them up to fight each other. The mermen glared at their dueling partners, more than willing to fight for the right to marry her.

"Let the best merman win!" Bree suddenly cried.

Bree hurried behind the open castle door. The mermen roared and began battling one another. She watched, feeling powerful but also a little sick to her stomach.

"What is going on here?" King Octopus demanded. The magnificently-dressed King exited the castle and looked upon his fighting guards with disdain. "Stop at once!"

The mermen ignored King Octopus' command. Bree's plan was working perfectly.

Carefully avoiding his eight long tentacles, Bree snuck past King Octopus and into his castle. Safely inside, she looked at the map Crystal Waters had given her. Following the instructions she had been given, Bree passed the main foyer, went up two flights of stairs and then entered the master bedroom. She studied the room, searching for the old wooden box. It was in that box, the queen had told her, that the diamond heart was hidden.

Bree had been searching for over ten minutes, but the box wasn't anywhere to be found. She felt her hope dwindle.

Suddenly, Bree heard a swishing noise. She knew a mermaid was approaching. Thinking quickly, Bree ducked under the bed. Her hip hit something. Looking down, she saw the old wooden box. Bree grabbed the box and then held her breath. The mermaid sounded closer and then faded.

Bree opened the box. Inside was the most beautiful diamond she had ever seen. The heart-shaped diamond sparkled with even the slightest move. Bree suddenly felt greedy. She wanted the diamond for herself.

*Don't do it,* her commonsense whispered to her. *Your life is worth more than any diamond.*

Bree held the diamond tightly as she squeezed through the window. She swam high above the guards, who were still feuding, and the frustrated king.

*Sometimes men can be so stupid.* She laughed to herself.


Tired but accomplished, Bree presented the diamond heart to Crystal Waters.

The queen grabbed it, not bothering to thank Bree. She placed the diamond heart in the middle of her golden spear. Crystal Waters held the golden spear high as it shimmered. A loud twinkling noise was then heard. It grew in intensity, causing Bree to cover her ears.

The sea swirled and everything around Bree began to melt together. In a few moments, she was breathlessly watching a scene unfold in front of her. The queen's castle rose from the chasm, replacing King Octopus' colony. He, along with the treacherous guards, were usurped from their castle.

Bree then swirled in another direction. She watched as Sandy, in human form, was dragged back into the sea. His legs began to transform into his original tail, while Bree regained her own legs. She let out a happy cry before everything went black.


Bree woke up on the sandy beach. She was lying face down and had to spit out a mouthful of water. It was now night. The beach was empty and everything was silent.

*The queen kept her promise.* Bree smiled to herself as she stood up. It felt funny walking on land again, but she was happy to be home.

Hurrying along the beach, she stopped only for a moment to see that the large shell, which Sandy had given her, was now gone.

*Good riddance,* Bree thought.

Bree entered the house to see Luke sitting on the couch with his head in his hands. He looked completely distraught. Upon hearing the door open, Luke looked up.

"Bree! Oh, Bree!" Luke ran to Bree and embraced her tightly. "Where have you been?"

She tried to laugh casually. "I was only gone for a day."

"I didn't know where you were. I thought something horrible had happened to you." Luke studied Bree's exhausted face. "*Did* something bad happen to you?"

"No."

Luke didn't look convinced. "Well," he sighed, "I'm always here for you. If you ever need to talk..."

"I know." Bree kissed Luke's cheek. "I'm going to wash up and then go to bed."

In the bathroom, Bree brushed her teeth. All the while she was thinking about her adventurous day. Even more important though was Luke's feelings for her.

*Luke's the best friend a girl could ever wish for,* Bree thought as she rinsed her mouth and then filled the sink.

Bree was about to wash her face when Crystal Waters appeared like a mirage in the sink. Shocked at seeing the queen once again, Bree gasped.

"Bree," Crystal Waters tittered. "Oh, Bree. I just want to thank you for bringing me up from the chasm. I forgot how much I love the warm water at the top of the sea. I could stay there forever, but I'd like to try something new."

Bree gulped and backed away from the sink.

"Bree," Crystal Waters continued in a hypnotizing voice. "Wouldn't you like to go for a little swim? Perhaps visit a sacred cavern?"

With all the strength she could gather, Bree lunged towards the sink and pulled the plug. The water, along with Crystal Waters' apparition, went down the drain.

*I think it's time to move,* Bree silently told herself.

* * *

## About the Author

Heather Beck is a Canadian author and screenwriter who began writing professionally at the age of sixteen. Her first book was published when she was only nineteen years old. Since then she has written several well-reviewed books.

Heather recently received an Honors Bachelor of Arts from university where she specialized in English and studied an array of disciplines. Currently, she is working on two young adult novels and has six anthologies slated for publication. As a screenwriter, Heather has multiple television shows and movies in development. Her short films include *Young Eyes* and *The Rarity*.

Besides writing, Heather's greatest passion is the outdoors. She is an award-winning fisherwoman and a regular hiker. Her hobbies include swimming, playing badminton and volunteering with non-profit organizations.